Hunting You

Warriors Series, Book 7

by

Ty Patterson

Acknowledgements

No book is a single person's product. I am privileged that Hunting You has benefited from the inputs of several great people.

Jean Coldwell, Claire Forgacs, Hank Halstead, Donald Hoffman, Richard Lane, Jim Lambert, Christine Terrell, Jack Willis, who are my beta readers and who helped shape my book, my launch team for supporting me, and Donna Rich for her editing and proofreading.

Books by Ty Patterson

Warriors Series

The Warrior, Warriors series, Book 1
The Reluctant Warrior, Warriors series, Book 2
The Warrior Code, Warriors series, Book 3
The Warrior's Debt, Warriors series, Book 4
Flay, Warriors series, Book 5
Behind You, Warriors series, Book 6
Hunting You, Warriors series, Book 7

Available on Amazon, Nook Books, Kobo and iTunes

Sign up to Ty Patterson's mailing list on his website, www. typatterson.com and get the ebook copy of The Warrior, free. Be the first to know about new releases and deals.

Dedications

To my parents, who taught me the value of a good education. My wife for her patience, and my son for listening to my jokes. To all my beta readers, my launch team, and well-wishers.
To all the men and women in uniform who make it possible for us to enjoy our freedoms.

'Never n the history of human conflict was so much owed by so many to so few.' Winston Churchill

Chapter 1

Herb 'Hank' Parker was having dinner with his family in Damascus, Virginia, when the masked men burst inside.

Hank had a small construction business that wasn't ever going to make him extraordinarily rich, but it fed his children and kept his family happy, which was all that really mattered.

Damascus had a population of less than a thousand people and crime was almost unheard of. There was that time when a few kids had set fire inside a trash can, but Hank couldn't remember the last time a home had been burgled or a murder had been committed.

There were three intruders, all of medium build, all brown or black-eyed; it was hard to see in the dining room's light.

The three flanked the dining room, one at its head, two at each side. Each one of them carried a handgun that was casually, but effectively held. Hank recognized that stance; these men were used to carrying and using handguns.

Petals, his six-year-old daughter, and Emily, his wife, started screaming on seeing the intruders. Nine-year-old Cody started hyperventilating.

Hank had been to Iraq in a special unit that did nasty stuff to the enemy. He had lived through a war that he never spoke of. Hank kept calm.

'There's some money in the safe in the bedroom,' he said evenly. 'My wallet's in the living room. There's some cash in it. We don't have any jewelry. Please take the cash and anything else you want. We won't offer any trouble.'

The hooded man at the head of the table looked at him in silence for a moment, then lifted his gun and shot Cody.

A full minute of silence fell in the room and then Emily started screaming; Petals heaved drily, her eyes wide and unseeing.

'No!' Hank left his seat like a rocket, his compact frame heaving the table to one side, his hands outstretched, reaching out for the nearest gunman, to rip his heart out.

A gun came crashing down on him and when he came to, he was tied to a chair, his wife and daughter similarly restrained, seated opposite him.

Petals seemed to have gone into a fugue; Emily's eyes were glazed and she was moaning softly.

'Where's the money you stole from Big G?' The masked

man asked in a tone that was almost bored. Hank shook his head woozily and when he looked at his son's body, it all came back to him. He turned to the masked man and tried to focus his eyes.

The man's accent was American, but beyond that Hank couldn't make out regional influences.

'Big G? I don't know him, man. I never stole any money from anyone.'

He strained against his bonds, but they were tight and there was no wriggle room. His wife's eyes flickered at the sound of his voice, but she didn't look his way. Petals was still out of it.

Thank the Lord for that.

He forced his body to wake up, stay alert and remain calm. *My family needs me.* He didn't look in Cody's direction.

'You got the wrong family, friend. Please take whatever money we have and leave.'

The masked hood crouched before him and Hank now saw his eyes were brown.

'Everyone starts off with a lie.'

The masked man nodded to one of his gunmen.

The screaming began.Ninety minutes later, Hank lay on his side, his insides spilling out. Death was hovering close by, waiting, hiding in the dark mist that was closing in on him.

His eyes stared dully on the floor; raising them was too much of an effort. If he lifted them he would've seen the bodies of his wife and daughter slumped on the floor.

A shadow moved, the hood knelt beside him and grabbed his hair and lifted his head. The man's face swam in Hank's vision but never focused.

'Now do you remember?'

The elevated angle brought his family into view and something primeval stirred within Hank. In its dying moments, his memory unfolded a face and a name.

A person that even death tiptoed around.

'Zebadiah Carter. He has the money.' Hank gasped out with his last breath and died with the hint of a smile on his face.

Zeb Carter would avenge his family's death.Big G paced the small cell of his high security prison in Guadalajara, Mexico when word got to him that Hank Parker had named some other man just before he died.

Big G was built like a tank, every inch of his body covered in tats. Muscles rippled when he walked and his black eyes bored holes into anyone he came across.

Nobody bothered him in the prison; heck, he ran it like his private office, any number of prisoners ready to do his bidding.

He had members of his gang in the prison, who relayed commands to the outside world, using a network of corrupt officials.

His gang ran like clockwork, even though Big G was incarcerated, living in a cell smaller than a bathroom in most American homes.

His clenched fists were knotted to the size of boxing gloves at the thought that he, Big G, was reduced to pacing like an animal in a cage.

All because of that snitch.Seven years ago, Big G was the undisputed criminal gang lord on the east coast of the United States.

Having split from the Killer Boos, a fast-growing inner city gang in Miami, Big G had built his criminal enterprise slowly, but surely, and always violently.

He bartered with those gangs he couldn't subdue, killed the leaders of those gangs smaller than his, acquired territory and became one of the most fearsome thugs on the eastern seaboard.

His gang marking was simple; a large G tattooed on every man's neck. Spray painted Gs on the walls of the territories they controlled.

His crew was over two hundred strong and was a major supplier of drugs from New Hampshire to Miami. His gang's reach extended to Chicago, Tennessee, and Atlanta, where he had chapters.

Big G didn't limit his business to narcotics alone, however. He also ran women and children in numerous cities and towns in that area. He dealt in stolen cars, laundered money and ran protection rackets.

The Feds were after him, as were numerous other law agencies, but not one could find him nor could they find anything on him.

That changed when a snitch spilled Big G's dealings and

whereabouts in return for witness protection.

Cezar, a dealer who ran the gang in Virginia, had been with Big G right from the Killer Boos days. He was part of the inner circle, trusted with everything, and spent time with Big G on a daily basis.

He had started changing when he had hooked up with a new woman. She wanted him to go straight and went about *reforming* him. She bombarded his ears every minute till Cezar couldn't take it any longer and went to the Feds.

Big G got wind of it and fled to Mexico, where he had connections, but the Federales over there were quick to act on a tip-off and grabbed him when he crossed the border.

Big G was carted off to the high security prison, where he still was.

Big G uncurled his fists and breathed deeply; slow calming breaths that some crackhead had taught him.

In. Pause. Out. In. Pause. Out.

The crackhead swore by deep breathing and said it balanced inner chakras, whatever the fuck they were.

Cezar. It was bad enough that he had turned snitch. He had also stolen thirty million dollars from the gang.

My money.

Big G's gang had started hunting him the moment the gang lord had established his supremacy and dominance in the prison. Over four years of establishing contacts and bribing people had finally paid off.

The gang got a contact in the Marshals service, which ran the witness protection program. The contact demanded a million dollars.

Big G authorized it. One mil in return for thirty? It was a no-brainer. More than the money, he wanted to lay his hands on Cezar and that bitch who had taken away his freedom.

The contact revealed that Cezar was now one Herb Parker, living in Damascus with his family and had quit the old ways.

Big G ordered his men to look into Parker and they dutifully reported that the timeline fit. Parker and his family were the right age.

They smuggled photographs in the prison and they were the clincher. Parker looked like Cezar. His wife looked like the bitch. That was enough for Big G.

He ordered the hit and, when his men reported that Cezar and his family had died, Big G closed his eyes for a moment.

They flashed open the next second when his man said they hadn't recovered the money.

Big G's eyes riddled the man in front of him and for a moment he was tempted to snap the criminal's scrawny neck.

His hood must have sensed his life was in danger for he spoke rapidly. Cezar had mentioned a name. He had said that person would have the money.

That man's name was Zebadiah Carter.

Big G tried to place the man. Nope, he hadn't heard of him. 'Find him. Find my money. Then kill him. Slowly.' He ordered and exited the cell.

He walked down the prison corridor enjoying the silence that fell when he approached.

Everyone feared him. Now this man, Carter, would feel his wrath.

Chapter 2

The killing made national headlines for a day and then politicians and vacuous celebrities took over the media.

In Washington D.C., a smartly-dressed man and woman sat opposite a grim faced elderly man.

The three of them didn't exchange words till an aide had served coffee and had departed silently. Both men had short hair, the older man's was streaked with grey, while the younger's black hair shone in the light. The woman had a ponytail that swung slightly whenever her body moved.

'Tell me you have something,' Bob Pierce, Deputy Director of the FBI glared at his agents.

Mark Kowalski looked at Sarah Burke, the senior agent of the two, whose face wore a frustrated expression. 'We haven't made much progress, sir. We traced the plates of the car that was seen outside their home. It was stolen in New Jersey from a drugstore parking lot. No one knows who stole it. There are no prints at the Parker residence. No trace evidence. No one saw anything, except the neighbor who noticed the out-of-state car and reported it.'

She stopped talking when Pierce looked away and trained his glare on the darkened windows that looked out on the street.

The FBI had gotten involved when the New Jersey plated car had been reported. Kowalski and Burke, part of a crack FBI team, had flown in with the rest of their crew and had taken over from the local and state police. Their investigation had hit a brick wall when they had found there was little evidence to process.

The national press might have forgotten the murders, but the state's media hadn't. The calls to the FBI Director came regularly from the Virginia Governor's office, once the Feds took over the investigation.

The state's two U.S. Senators and eleven Congressmen piled on the pressure, and three months from the killing, Pierce called in the two agents. To discuss the murder, his assistant had told the agents, but they all knew it was to let them know the heat he was feeling.

Burke and Kowalski left his office an hour later, headed to the nearest coffee shop where the male agent ordered an extra large drink and downed it rapidly. Burke smiled slightly when he put down his mug.

'Pierce was in a good mood.'

The smile broke into a chuckle at Kowalski's incredulous look. 'That was just his bark. You haven't seen him bite.'

Burke, born and grown up in the Bronx, came from a law enforcement family. Her father rode a patrol car in New York; her grandfather had been a beat cop, her mother worked at the NYPD's call center. The NYPD had been a natural home for her, where she too had started out in a patrol car.

Her intelligence, hard work, and ambition secured her the rank of detective first grade, which was when she had applied to the FBI. She passed her training at Quantico with flying colors and came to the attention of the Deputy Director who was putting together his task force, an elite team of investigators,

Pierce monitored her career for three years and when she kept acing all her cases, invited her to head the unit. He broke protocol in doing so, rubbed several egos the wrong way, but he trusted his instincts. In the four years that Sarah Burke had headed the task force, she had never let him down.

Till The Parker Murders, as the state media had taken to calling the case.

Kowalski, a lawyer by qualification, had joined the FBI as a trainee agent and after his graduation, had joined the unit just a year back. He was bright, smart, and had serious potential; which explained why he was being mentored by Burke.

He wiped his mouth with a napkin and glanced at her curiously. 'Why didn't you tell him about the murders in New Jersey?'

A lone man had been murdered in New Jersey, a couple of weeks after the Damascus killings.

The killing attracted Burke's interest when she noticed the mutilations on the body were similar to those on the Parkers. On top of that, the man was similar in looks to Hank Parker. She had flown to New Jersey and on studying the crime scene had taken the investigation under the FBI's fold. Burke had juice; her track record ensured that.

'We don't have anything on it either, at least for the Deputy Director, at this moment.' Her eyes smiled. 'We could go back to him right now, however, if you want to experience his bite.' Kowalski threw his hands up in surrender and the matter was settled.

Burke paid for their drinks, threw in a hefty tip and braced herself mentally before hitting the street. She had closed many difficult investigations, but this one had a different feel to it.

This one could get messy.

A second later, a bleak thought entered her mind. *It has to go somewhere to get messy. That seems a remote possibility at the moment.*

Sarah Burke didn't know it but there was another person who had taken an interest in her investigation.Zeb Carter was in Libya, had been there for six months, when Hank was killed. Zebadiah 'Zeb' Carter worked for an U.S. agency that no one knew of. The Agency was headed by a gray-eyed, icy cool woman who had risen to be its Director and who reported to only one person. The President of the United States.

The Agency took out terrorists, international war criminals, and those who trafficked in humans and drugs. It recovered missing nuclear and chemical weapons, neutralized despots and buried threats to the country's security.

Its budget was hidden in a complex financial maze and Clare, the Director, held an insignificant position in those corridors of power that ran Washington D.C. Less than a handful of people knew of the Agency's existence and even fewer knew Clare's specific role.

Clare, wanting to reduce the Agency's administrative footprint to near zero, had looked at several means and had discarded all of them. She had come across Zeb Carter while having dinner with a close friend of hers; she had initially thought the man lounging outside the restaurant was her friend's boyfriend.

The man was clean-shaven, lean, a shade over six feet and had brown hair that was cut short. His eyes were dark; he was casually dressed in a white shirt over blue jeans and looked unremarkable to the ordinary eye.

Clare's experienced gaze noted the stillness in him, the way people on the sidewalk parted in silent acknowledgement of him, and the liquid ease in his movements.

Her friend noticed her glance, looked in the man's direction and laughed loudly when Clare asked if the man was her boyfriend.

'Zeb is my brother. Major Zebadiah Carter, though he isn't in the army anymore.'

'He's a mercenary, a private military contractor,' she added when Clare crooked her brow inquisitively.

The laugh bubbled out again at the look on Clare's face. 'It isn't the money he's chasing. He doesn't need more; he's done very well for himself. That man outside is the most principled man you will ever come across. He's also the most dangerous.'

Clare had known her friend, Cassandra, her friend, for decades. Having started off as roommates in Bryn Mawr, the two had pursued careers in the nation's capital, and their bond had only grown stronger as their careers progressed. Clare knew Cassandra wasn't given to hyperbole.

She checked out Major Zebadiah Carter's file and found that it was redacted. Her security clearance gave her access to the unedited version, and on reading it, she knew she had found the first operative for the Agency in its new avatar.

Zeb Carter had been a Special Forces operative, had been to almost every hotspot in the world where he had worked on deep black missions. Awards and honors filled his file: Purple Heart, Distinguished Service Cross, Medal of Honor. From other countries too. Letters of commendations were part of the file. His commanding officers had been fulsome in their praise and had tried their best to get him to remain in the Army.

There was some detail on his career after leaving the Army. He had worked as a military contractor but only on those assignments that met his strict code. No missions that threatened national security. No war on women or children.

After a few years as a mercenary, he had set up a security consulting business in New York that advised corporations, entrepreneurs and celebrities. She looked for, and found details of his family, and exhaled slowly when she read them.

Major Zebadiah Carter was a loner. He hadn't always been so.

She called a few Pentagon generals and all of them had nothing but praise for him. She had already made her mind up to contact Zeb; however, she waited to have lunch with one last general.

General Daniel Klouse was no ordinary general; he was the National Security Advisor to the President. He knew of the Agency's existence and supported Clare in the rare political battles she had to fight. His bushy eyebrows had come together when she asked him about Zeb.

'Are you seeking him or is he after you?'

He smiled grimly when she paused. 'It makes a difference. If he's after you, nothing can save you. Nothing.'

She looked in the eyes of one of the most powerful men in the country and believed him.

She called Zeb Carter the next day and made him an offer. He heard her out politely and to her surprise, turned her down.

He then made a counter offer – he would continue working in his security consulting business, but only as a cover. In reality the Agency would be his employer, but this disguise would give her the small footprint she desired, as well as deniability. He would hire other mercenaries to form the rest of his crew; again, all of them would be his firm's employees.

He and his crew would be free to take on other assignments on the understanding that the Agency's missions came first and all such assignments would be vetted by Clare.

He then presented Broker to her.

Broker, an ex-Ranger, was an intelligence analyst who had worked in the Army; his smarts and lateral thinking had brought him to the notice of those who made decisions. He had risen relatively fast and high in the Army, but its rules had finally stifled him and he had left to set up his own intelligence business.

That business had flourished; it had analysts all over the world who submitted daily reports to Werner, a highly sophisticated artificial intelligence program that ran in Zeb's office in New York.

Werner collated the analysts' reports, overlaid them with the data it had mined from the internet, and sent out briefs to Broker's clients the world over. The clients included global companies, national governments, politicians, several national and international police forces and government intelligence organizations.

Clare ran Broker past the NSA and the Pentagon; both organizations and several generals rated him highly. She cleared his appointment. By now she knew how Zeb worked and had begun to trust him implicitly.

Zeb came back to her with a list of names, his crew. She went through their files and hid a smile of satisfaction.

All of them had been some of the best operatives while in the Army; now they freelanced in the private sector. Bwana, Roger, Bear, and Chloe were the initial recruits, all of them ex-Special Forces except Chloe who had been with the 82nd

Airborne.

Beth and Meghan Peterson, twins, had joined this initial team, later on. The twins, originally businesswomen from Boston, had been rescued by Zeb from a gang of assassins in an earlier mission. They had gravitated toward the quiet man, their savior, and had requested to join his team.

Zeb had refused point blank. The Agency was no place for the twins.

The Petersons changed tack. They badgered Broker till they broke his resistance and got him to convince Zeb; they then relocated to New York and now ran the operations for the Agency.

Broker, in his late forties, was the oldest of them, but he was in good shape and with his looks, passed for a decade younger.

The twins, in their late twenties, were the youngest. The rest of them were in their late thirties.

Zeb was their leader, Broker the second in command, but they didn't have a real hierarchy.

The eight of them worked as one, a smoothly functioning unit that the President had once jestingly called, Clare's Warriors.

The name stuck.

Chapter 3

At the moment Hank died, Zeb had been urging his goats, fifty of them, to cross a dry wadi in northeast Libya.

The other side of the wadi had a few sparse bushes, on which the animals could feed, and a well from which they could drink.

It was midday, the sun beat down on them mercilessly, and his goats were cranky and stubborn, but he was patient.

He clicked his tongue, urged the leaders to pick up the pace and with a few flicks of the stick in his hand, the herd moved slowly, trotting across the softer bed of the wadi.

Nothing else moved in the gorge where he was, but for him and his animals.

The gorge was part of the Akhdar Mountains, also known as the Green Mountains, that rose gradually from the surrounding flat land in Libya and became part of the Jabal al Akhdar plateau that, at its highest point, was nearly three thousand feet above sea level.

The mountains received a fair amount of rainfall compared to the rest of the country and livestock herding was commonplace.

There was limited agriculture; farms that produced olives, grapes, and almonds. Such farming had received a boost from better irrigation; but it was camel, goat, and sheep herds that were most commonly seen in the mountains.

Bayda was the nearest city where the animals would be sold.

It was the capital of the mountainous district, and had all the trappings of a commercial city, but it was caught in a war between ISIS, which had a hold in parts of the country, and the various Libyan militias opposing it.

The deposal and subsequent killing of Gaddafi had left a vacuum in Libya, which ISIS had been quick to capitalize on. By the time the western world had woken up to the ISIS threat in that country, it was too late.

The terrorists had grabbed Derna, a city to the northeast of the mountains and while Derna had been wrested back by the Libyan militias, the battle between the two forces had spread across the country.

Zeb was hunting Beslan Umkhayey, a Chechen terrorist who

was running an ISIS training camp in northern Libya.

The hunt had been tortuous; there wasn't any hard evidence other than whispers of a secretive camp in the country where young men with extremist ideologies from all over the world, were trained by a brutal man.

The Agency had worked with the NSA, the CIA, as well as other acronymed agencies, and a clearer picture began to emerge after piecing together the various rumors.

Umkhayey was a wanted terrorist in Chechnya but had fled that country when the heat on him had become unbearable.

He had surfaced in a few ISIS videos in Syria but had subsequently disappeared.

Intelligence agencies thought he had died; after all, terrorists had a short shelf life.

Then the rumors began surfacing. There was a new training camp in Libya. Run by a short, European-looking, bearded man. A man who bore a resemblance to Umkhayey.

Surveillance planes flew over the country, chatter was monitored and Werner worked with other supercomputers to listen for elusive words.

The puzzle became clearer when an ISIS fighter was captured in Mosul and, with his dying words mentioned Umkhayey and Libya in the same breath.

The mission came to the Agency and led to Zeb parachuting into the Libyan Desert, six months back.

Zeb landed fifty miles from the base of the mountains and, after hiding his gear, started his life as Nasser Ayyad, a goat herder who had lost his family, which was everything, in a bombing in the city of Taknis.

Arabic came easy to Zeb; he had been undercover in the Middle East several times and could speak the language fluently in several dialects, with the appropriate accents.

His skin was tanned and blended easily with the Libyan populace.

He darkened his hair and now, with the long white shirt, loose trousers, and occasional white headdress as garb, Nasser Ayyad roamed the country.

He worked as an animal herder, a handyman, helped rebuild bombed-out houses, carried old men on his back, anything that brought him in contact with people.

He listened a lot, spoke little, smiled easily and it was in the hostile city of Derna that he heard the first suggestion of a training base high in the mountains.

He walked miles in the night to escape the burning heat of the day, joined camp with livestock herders in the night and shared bread and milk with them.

Occasionally he was accosted by the Libyan militias or groups of terrorists.

Nasser Ayyad had a good cover and his ready smile and the offer of a goat dispelled any suspicion. He didn't look white. No one suspected him of coming from the Great Satan's country.

Days and nights rolled into one blur and became months and then Zeb had his first sight of the camp.

It was high up as the rumors had mentioned. It consisted of fifty tents crudely lined up in concentric circles with the outermost circle holding the guards, the innermost ones housing the recruits.

Around the camp, which covered several acres, were sentries who looked like they would shoot first and ask questions later.

They didn't detect the man buried under loose soil; they didn't see the earth-colored breathing tube that poked a few millimeters above ground.

Some of the sentries had elaborate counter-surveillance equipment. They had radio jammers, NVGs (Night Vision Goggles), and Zeb spotted a thermal imager in one sentry's hands.

None of them spotted him. The specially designed skintight anti-reflective wrap around him eluded thermal detectors. He crawled closer to the camp when he could, either in the day or the night. Most of the time he lay buried in dugouts that he built.

On any other mission he would have sent a drone up and got it to capture the camp; on this one, he just had to use his phone which had a specially modified camera that could take long range, still or video shots.

The phone had a battery that could go for weeks without charging. It was the only high-tech gadget that he had on his body.

One month after coming across the camp, he spotted Umkhayey.

The Chechen was walking outside the perimeter of tents, arguing with two of his guards. The height was right, the beard was right, and when the man's face turned to catch the light, the features were right.

The camera captured the terrorist from several angles and at night, when the forest slept, a short burst of encrypted data went up in the sky, linked to a satellite, and made its way to Clare's computer.

A week later, a message came back to Zeb.

Take him out.

Zeb rested his head on a pillow shaped from dried goat droppings, stared at the stars that returned his gaze unblinkingly.

He started making plans.

Can't go into the camp. It would be suicidal. It has to be outside.

He circled the camp slowly for ten days and detected their supply route.

It was a track that went through the thick of the forest, wended down the mountains, wound across a dusty and barren plain and joined a highway that went to Derna.

Once a week, a truck rumbled through the camp, carrying food, ammunition, clothing and more recruits.

Two Jeeps, stuffed with men, flanked the truck at either end and protected it from attack. The three vehicles bore the international symbols of hospital vehicles.

To fool overhead surveillance.

Zeb took pictures, hundreds of them, of the camp, of the recruits, of the guards, and sent them back to the Agency.

Analysts would pore over those images, piece together the bios of the men and many of them would go on various black lists maintained by Western worlds.

A black list was a kill list. Every ally maintained one, though they all stoutly denied the existence of such lists.

Zeb got his break in a few days.

A closed Jeep went out of the camp every couple of weeks with just three men in it. Two of them were guards; one of whom doubled as the driver as well. The third man was short and wore a headdress that came low over his forehead.

Zeb had noted the vehicle and its contents before, but this time he got a better glimpse of the man in the headdress.

A gust of wind blew and lifted the covering away and underneath, Umkhayey's beard and burning eyes were revealed.

The Jeep followed the track out of the forest, across the

plain, disappeared on the road to Derna and returned late in the evening.

Maybe an opportunity on the road?

It took Zeb ten days to move away from the camp and head down to the plains and once there, he buried himself near the highway and waited for the arrival of the vehicle.

It came four days later, passing no more than fifty yards from him. The driver glanced idly in his direction but saw only bush and sand and soil.

The passenger next to him turned back and laughed at someone in the back.

Umkhayey.

Zeb saw him through the windows on the rear. The Chechen had discarded his headdress and had his arms outstretched on the bench seat in the back.

Traffic was sparse on the highway; not many Libyans were desperate to head to war-torn Derna.

Those who could, had escaped the city a long while ago. Those who couldn't, were stuck there, caught between opposing factions, living their life in perpetual uncertainty.

The Jeep returned late at night, its twin beams piercing through the darkness, separating dirt track from the rest of the plains.

Zeb could have taken out the three passengers, if he hadn't been buried in his hide.

He extracted himself from the dugout the next day, walked five miles and re-joined his goats.

He greeted Omar and Abdul, two other goat herders he had befriended several months back and who had been looking after his animals in his absence.

Omar and Abdul were in their twenties and had been looking after livestock for as long as they could remember.

They were from the southern part of the country, and had left their villages to seek a better life and that quest had brought them to be with Zeb.

The three of them together had close to a hundred goats; the animals were close by, bedded down for the night.

The three goat herders shared warm milk and bread and told outrageous tales and lay awake late in the night.

Omar asked Zeb about his visit to Derna; his cover story was that he was seeking relatives whose last known address

25

was in that city.

Zeb shrugged; his relatives' home was rubble now. He had spent months in the city but he had come no closer to knowing if they were alive or dead.

He had witnessed bombings and shootings and was once caught in a crossfire. He was lucky to be alive. Silence fell over them as the two younger men stared into the fire that danced orange and red.

Zeb asked them if anything exciting had happened in his absence.

Omar chuckled. A dust storm had scattered their herd and it had taken days to recover the lost animals.

They settled down for the night and when his companions were fast asleep, Zeb rose silently, skirted the animals and briskly walked for two miles. His arms cache was buried under a lone bush in the desert.

He retrieved a Glock, a Benchmade, spare magazines and something that looked like putty.

The putty was an explosive that could be molded to any shape and could withstand the desert heat. He withdrew detonators and batteries, then covered the rest of his cache and headed back to his camp.

During the next week, he nudged their herds closer to the track Umkhayey's Jeep would take.

Omar and Abdul went along when he mentioned better grazing. The two men had a cheerful outlook and nothing much darkened their brows.

The days were spent in idly patrolling their herd, finding shade to eat and rest under, and playing cards.

Card games and spinning yarns occupied their time. They talked about going to a nearby city and selling some of their goats, but the animals needed to be fattened up first.

The day before Umkhayey headed out, Zeb deliberately and unobtrusively scattered their combined herd.

The three of them spent the entire day scouring the plains for their animals and by the time dusk fell, the younger men were exhausted.

They rolled up in their bedding after a quick dinner and when Zeb heard them snoring, he rose and silently packed his few belongings. He wasn't worried about the men waking; the sedative he had inserted in their milk would keep them asleep for over fifteen hours.

He urged the goats to move and after several prods, the lead animals rose and plodded in the direction he steered. Umkhayey's driver roared in laughter at a crude joke the Chechen made.

He was in high spirits; their fortnightly visit to Derna was to indulge themselves in food, drink, and experience the pleasures of a prostitute.

The training of terrorists was exhausting and they deserved a break. The prostitute knew they were coming. She didn't like them, but that made it all the more enjoyable for the men.

It was barely midday, but the sun was already a bright yellow disc high above, and beat down on them mercilessly.

The plains were empty, the highway was clear, an unwilling woman was waiting, the world was theirs.

The first goat came out of a small dip in the ground and sauntered right in front of them.

The driver cursed, swerved and yelled at the animal, which bleated back in return.

A second goat came on the track, then a third, and soon the track was filled by animals aimlessly milling around.

The driver tried counting them and gave up when he reached fifty. Their hoofs raised a small dust storm that blew toward them and surrounded them.

The driver peered out of the door, a hand partially covering his face and yelled out in the silence.

Where was the goat herder? Didn't he know better?

He turned back to Umkhayey who asked him who he was shouting at.

The goat herder obviously, he replied, controlling his irritation.

The passenger peered out too and spotted the figure in white who had appeared from the same dip in the road.

'Clear the track, you fool,' he roared at the man.

The goat herder bobbed his head in acknowledgment, approached the jeep and ducked suddenly.

The passenger leaned out further to spot him, one hand carelessly gripping his AK47.

He uttered something undecipherable and his body slid out of the jeep and disappeared behind the vehicle's canopy.

The driver sounded his horn repeatedly, but the animals didn't budge, the goat herder didn't turn up.

Neither did the passenger.

27

Umkhayey was irritated. He had a date with a woman and a herd of dumb animals was delaying him.

He poked his head out of the door and saw a sea of grey animals. No human.

He shouted and when he got no reply in response, a frown crept across his face. He scanned the rear, the front, gestured at the driver to look out from his side.

Nothing. Nothing moved on the plains, other than the animals, milling around. Some of them relieved themselves and the stench seeped inside the vehicle.

The driver put a foot out of the jeep and prepared to step down from the vehicle, his rifle at the ready, when a shout emerged from the rear of the herd and the white robed figure of the goat herder appeared.

He waved a stick and swatted at the animals but all that did was push them closer to the jeep.

One of them defecated near the driver. He scrambled back inside and his voice rose in fury and a stream of curses flew at the herder.

The white robed man raised his hands in pleading, as if to say, help me.

Umkhayey spat in disgust. 'Help him.'

The driver stepped out gingerly and fired out a warning burst in the air.

The animals on his side scattered and a clear space emerged. The herder requested him to come to the back and similarly help clear those animals.

'Am I your helper?' The driver cursed angrily but went to the rear.

Umkhayey fidgeted in his seat, glanced at his watch and peered out from the passenger side.

An animal stared at him balefully and bleated scornfully.

'Veseli? Besmir?' He called out to the driver and the passenger.

There was no acknowledgement.

Alarm filled him.

He crawled over the passenger seat and stepped out, every nerve on alert, his black eyes scanning over the heads of the animals.

A slight breeze kicked up the dust further and surrounded the jeep.

He cupped his left hand over the lower part of his face and

his eyes narrowed when the white robed figure rose suddenly.

'What's happening? Where are my men?' His rifle swung toward the herder in a slow arc.

The robed man stepped closer.

The herder came nearer, moving impossibly fast, faster than the swing of Umkhayey's rifle.

Umkhayey lowered his left hand, changing his grip on the AK47, and started bringing it up.

Still the herder came, just a few feet away and now the Chechen saw his eyes for the first time.

Brown. Dark brown. Cold. Narrowed to a pinpoint. The herder's face was hard angles and narrowed in focus.

Something leapt in Umkhayey. This was no animal herder.

His finger depressed the trigger. The shots went wide and high when an arm as hard and unyielding as a steel bar brushed the barrel up and away, almost carelessly.

Umkhayey let go of the AK47 and leapt at the robed man, one hand scrabbling inside his loose robe for his handgun.

He never reached the man.

Something pierced him. Something hard and shining.

He stared down in surprise and saw it was a blade. It slid inside his chest with ease as if slicing through butter.

He grasped the wrist that was holding it, but it was firm. Unmoving, as if it was part of the blade.

The knife slide out and slid in again.

Umkhayey fell on the ground, struggled to get up, fell again when a boot was planted on him and the blade entered again.

Dust filled his mouth and nose, his vision started blurring.

Something splattered across his face. He opened his eyes with great effort and his last sight was of a goat urinating near him. Zeb wiped the Benchmade and slid it inside his robe.

His original plan had been to approach the vehicle and take the three men out.

The passenger's stepping out had crimped his plan but luckily the man had come forward unsuspectingly when Zeb beckoned him.

He had gone down easily, but the driver had put up more resistance.

Zeb dragged the bodies and laid them alongside one another.

He snapped several pictures on his phone and climbed into the driver's seat, reversed the vehicle, turned it around and drove away slowly through the milling animals.

The three bodies grew smaller in his mirror and then vanished.

They were caught unaware. They would have been ready for drones, for snipers, for armed vehicles.

They weren't expecting goats.

Chapter 4

Three days later a video surfaced on the internet and spread like wildfire throughout the Middle East and then across the rest of the social media addicted world.

It was from a masked man known as The Butcher of the Middle East.

The Butcher claimed to be a Taliban fighter who had taken it upon himself to rid the world of the traitorous ISIS.

The Taliban and the ISIS had an uneasy relationship; till the time the latter came along, the former ruled the roost as the primary terrorist threat to the world.

ISIS's brutal ascendance had attracted a wide following however, causing many discontented Taliban commanders and foot soldiers to join them.

No one knew who The Butcher was.

He was always masked and whenever he released a video it was with the Taliban's flag as a backdrop.

He spoke Arabic with an Iraqi accent, made long speeches about the evils of the ISIS and their cowardly ways.

This video contained more than a speech.

It showed pictures of the dead Umkhayey and his companions.

The Butcher gloated that he had gone into enemy territory and killed the men while ISIS conducted their killings from behind the safety of their armies.

The Taliban disowned The Butcher and said the killer did not belong to them.

No one believed them.Zeb scrubbed away the dyes on his face and hair, while he showered in the bathroom of his apartment in Jackson Heights.

His serious face stared back at him in the mirror when he was toweling dry, a face that seldom smiled, and to which laughter rarely came.

His friends ribbed him about his lack of humor. They said the Sphinx was more talkative.

He finger combed his short brown hair and dressed casually in a blue T-shirt over jeans.

He fired up his sat-phone, in order to check up on his messages.

There weren't many.

His crew didn't bother him when he was in hostile country and Clare emailed him rarely.

He sent a message to all of them announcing his return and when the flood of messages started pouring in, the hardness fell away from his face and a grin crept across his face

His silences gave his crew ample ammunition for their joshing and they never lost an opportunity to have a dig at him.

He slung a jacket over his shoulders and stepped outside in the sound and traffic snarl that was New York.

He breathed deeply the unique smell of exhaust, along with the sound of swearing and smiled briefly.

He was home.Zeb was The Butcher.

He had created that avatar during a previous mission and it had proved very successful in creating divisions between the two terror organizations.

Divisions that the Western world used to win back not only territory but also the minds and hearts of those susceptible to extremist propaganda.

Two days later Zeb was in Milton Mills, New Hampshire, in a small cottage that he owned. It was set back from the street, with just one other home as his nearest neighbor.

The small village was where he went after missions. It was where he unwound and let life wash over him.

Milton Mills had no more than three hundred residents, was contained in the larger town of Milton, and its proximity to the Salmon Falls River was what had made him fall in love with it.

The river once provided power to mills and factories on its bank.

Today it was a haven for kayakers and paddlers, who could navigate the river's lush shore and forget that there was a world beyond.

Zeb spent many hours on the river, when he was in the village. He liked the way time slowed when he was in Milton Mills.

Like many small neighborhoods in the country, the village was one where neighbors greeted and helped each other.

It had a mix of older residents and young families, all of who took enormous pride in their small town.

Zeb had been exploring the east coast, often kayaking through the several rivers and lakes, when he had come across

Milton Mills.

He had taken in the spaced out homes, many of them white or blue fronted, the simple, soaring church, and he had known immediately.

This was where he would come to decompress.

After researching the village, he found his small cottage; residents knew him as a businessman who escaped to their town for R&R every few months in a year.

They respected his need for solitude.

Pike, the balding, sixty-year-old resident who ran the local convenience store, was the one who had interacted with him the most.

'Which isn't saying much,' Pike waved his empty mug at Chuck, the bartender in their neighborhood watering hole, and turned back to his friends.

'He comes maybe once a week, when he's in the village, greets me, stocks up, pays, and leaves.'

'He minds his own business, doesn't play loud music, doesn't drive rashly, and is always polite. What more can one ask?' Bundy's cloudy eyes rested on each of them and got answering nods in return.

Bundy had bushy eyebrows and thick, white frizzy hair.

He was retired, a widower, and helped out in the village. He carried out repairs in the church, helped fix boilers, started recalcitrant cars, cleared snow and slush from sidewalks, and repaired broken windows.

Bundy was your man if you had a problem with your home, your car, or anything mechanical or inanimate.

Chuck was the silent type. Burly, round faced, he had a ready smile for patrons, but unlike other bartenders, he didn't indulge in small talk.

Sure, he gave directions when passing visitors asked, but he didn't probe, didn't push. He let his customers enjoy his hospitality without inflicting his presence on them.

Pike, Bundy, and Chuck were close.

Heck, they were like the founding fathers of the village and took enormous pride in the well being of their neighborhood.

Pike and Bundy and a few others met each evening at Chuck's, the only act in the village, and discussed worldly matters that also included events of the day.

Chuck brought refills to their table and when the men had fueled and lubricated themselves, they moved onto discussing the ball game.

Zeb's arrival in the village, years back, had sparked off gossip and rumors, which died away when he became a semi-permanent fixture in the town.

Residents saw him going for early morning runs and his neighbor, Jenny Wade, said the only time she was aware of his presence was when he undertook repairs to his home, or polished his kayak.

Jenny herself came to the village five years back, a baby in tow, but now called it home and fit in the small community like a comfortable glove.

Jenny's backyard was separated from Mr. Carter's by a thick, tall hedge. She could see over it into his yard, but she seldom saw him.

There was that time when he had hired a digger, one of those big things that removed earth, and had dug out his backyard.

That was strange, she said. He worked a lot at night and she never got to see what he was building. The backyard looked the same as before, when the digger had done its job.

In general the consensus was that while Mr. Carter cut a distinctly aloof figure, he was a part of their town and as such, deserved the same hospitality and warmth that the other residents got.Zeb's cottage was small. Two stories. A ground floor with a few rooms, an upper floor with a few more.

The ground floor had a living room, kitchen, dining room, a bedroom – which he had turned into a study – and a bathroom.

He had turned the dining room into an exercise room. It didn't have any equipment other than a skipping rope, a yoga mat, a punching bag, and a few weights.

The upper floor had three bedrooms, a bathroom, and a large landing space.

Two of the upper bedrooms looked down to his backyard and the hedge separating Jenny Wade's yard from his.

He could see the corner of the Wade house and a few of its windows, if he moved closer to his window.

His house was spartan in its decoration and other than a TV and a router, it had no other electronic equipment of its own.

The equipment that he required for his job was stored in a basement, some of it was kept in his SUV.

He had caches across the house, the yard, and the roof.

Zeb spent the first week of his arrival tidying up the front and the backyard and repairing some broken shingles on the roof.

He was aware of his neighbor's daughter peering at him from her upper story window and when he went to his front yard, she came out and watched him silently.

He mowed the lawn, picked litter, and stray leaves.

She joined him. She rubbed her tiny hand against her dress when they had finished and thrust it out at him.

'Olivia Wade,' she introduced herself, her blue eyes peering up at him through locks of golden hair.

'Zeb Carter.' He bent down and shook her hand. *She must be five or six years old.*

'Your mom knows you're here?'

Her hair bounced on her shoulders as she shook her head vigorously and darted away when a voice called out from her house.

He looked at his hand. There had been a time when small hands such as Olivia Wade's, had curled trustingly around his.

He broke the thought.A few days later, Zeb was in Chuck's bar, sampling the day's special, idling riffling through the pages of a week old newspaper.

He read the sports news, moved to the political section and caught up on which leader said what about whom, spent time on a couple of articles on Iraq and Syria and when he was pushing the paper away, he spotted the photograph.

It featured a smiling man surrounded by his family. A man whose face hadn't changed much in more than a decade except for the thinning hair and the fine layer of wrinkles around his eyes and mouth

Zeb was very familiar with that man; he had been Zeb's commander and mentor in a distant land, in which both men had lost many friends and had formed new bonds.

Zeb had shared stories with him over a campfire, had felt the man's hand on his shoulder when Zeb lost it, on seeing the body of a friend.

'Make sure you've folks in your life, boy. Life isn't meant for living alone.' The man used to say.

'You okay, Mr. Carter?' The voice came from far away and when it grew insistent, the mists of time dissipated and Zeb looked up in Chuck's face.

He realized he had been staring at the bar, seeing nothing, hearing a seldom visited past.

'Yeah, thanks.' He rose, dropped a few bills on the table and brushed past the bartender without a further word.

He turned back abruptly, picked up the paper and walked out, feeling Chuck's eyes boring into his back.

He hurried to his cottage and in its privacy, read the article again and then fired up his laptop and pored through all the available coverage.FBI Director Pat Murphy took the call two hours later and leaned back in his chair when he heard the voice on the other end of the line.

He listened silently for a moment, grunted, 'Hold,' and jabbed a button on his phone.

'Who's handling the Parker murders?' He asked his assistant when a grey-haired woman entered his office.

'Sarah Burke, she heads Bob Pierce's new task force.'

He waved in thanks and returned to the call and mentioned the names. He wasn't surprised when the voice asked where Sarah Burke could be found.

'Can I ask your interest in this case?'

The voice spoke briefly and Murphy nodded unconsciously. He understood now.

'Let me make some calls. I'll get back to you.'

Pat Murphy headed the premier investigative agency in the country.

He had thousands of agents at his beck and call. Senators and Congressmen vied to meet him. The President listened attentively when he spoke.

He would drop whatever was on his plate for Zeb Carter. They had history.

He rang Pierce's number and looked blindly at the rain blurring his office windows as the soft burrs went over the phone lines.

His Deputy Director picked on the fifth ring.

'Pat, yeah, how can I help?'

His voice was breathless as if he was running. Murphy glanced at the clock. Six p.m. It was when Pierce hit the treadmill in his office.

The Director was succinct and waited for the response he knew would come. It didn't take long.

'She's a good investigator, Pat. If there's anyone who can

crack this case, it's her. We shouldn't allow any interference.'

'He just wants to meet. He wants to see her in person and get a feel for her. I know him well. It's the way he works.'

'He'll want updates on her progress?' The question was sharp.

'Nope. Like I said, he wants to meet and assure himself that it's in good hands.'

'It is. She's the best. You know that.'

Murphy didn't reply and let the silence drag on and smiled briefly when Pierce capitulated and told him where Burke could be found.

'He won't interfere?' Pierce tried one last time.

'Nope.'

Pat Murphy could have gotten hold of Sarah Burke's number and given it to Zeb, but he liked to go through the chain of command.

It existed for a reason. It sent the wrong message if he, the director, went around it.

Burke and Kowalski were still in D.C. later that day, after being chewed out by Pierce.

They were on their phones in their hotel rooms, urging, cajoling, pleading, requesting, doing everything they could to get their team to find that elusive thread that would break the case open.

Burke hung her phone up an hour later, showered quickly, knocked on Kowalski's room, and went down to the lobby.

They had early morning flights the next day and the plan was to have an early dinner and a good sleep.

Kowalski joined her fifteen minutes later and they silently caught a cab to Georgetown, to a restaurant Burke frequented.

A wine glass later, the weight of the investigation had fallen away.

They made small talk, talked about Kowalski's fiancée, about New York, but the investigation wasn't far away.

Kowalski, cutting through his steak, brought it up. 'What if we don't find a lead?' He knew of Burke's record.

Burke shrugged. 'We'll move onto other cases.'

'Why won't you find a lead?'

Burke froze, her mouth half open, her fork poised in midair and stared at the lean man who had appeared at their table.

'This is a private dinner, pal. Can you leave us alone?'

Kowalski's smile was pleasant but through it, steel showed.

The man didn't reply. He reached back, dragged a chair from another table and seated himself at their table.

Burke tamped down a sudden surge of anger and her voice was controlled when she spoke. 'You heard what he said. Leave us. Forget what you heard.'

Her phone buzzed, she ignored it. She locked eyes with the man for the first time; his brown eyes reminded her of a roiling ocean.

The phone buzzed again.

'Take it,' he said and the fury sparked in her.

'Like hell –'

He picked her phone, thumbed the call accept and handed it to her.

His gall incensed her. She grabbed it from his hand, ready to do damage, when she heard the voice on the line and settled back in her seat.

'Yes, sir, he's with me.'

Pat Murphy spoke for a few minutes and when he had finished she dropped the phone on her table and got her composure back.

'The Director,' she answered the questioning look in Kowalski's eyes.

She turned back to the man at their table. 'The director says you have an interest in this case. Lots of people have an interest in several cases. What makes you special?'

Zeb Carter didn't reply. He glanced once at her phone and then at her and a wave of red spread across her face.

Pat Murphy called me. That's what makes him special.

She briefed him rapidly on where they were with the case, his eyes never leaving hers, and when she had finished, waited for a response.

None came. He sat still and when the silence became unbearable, Kowalski told Carter of the other murder.

The one in New Jersey.

Burke could read people. She was trained to detect tics on the face, involuntary gestures, narrowing of eyes, whitening of fingers, all kinds of giveaways.

She spotted nothing in Carter. She thought he seemed to still, a slowing of his metabolism, but she couldn't be sure.

The brown eyes moved to Kowalski and he elaborated on the details.

The waiter came to take Carter's order, he waved him away. The silence became thick and then he rose.

Like a panther rising, she thought.

'Thank you,' he said and walked away without another word.

Her mouth gaped open again and when she'd recovered, she called out. 'That's it? No, *keep me in the loop*? No, *call me when you find something*?'

He turned around once and smiled but didn't say anything.

'Just who are you, Mr. Carter?' Kowalski called out.

In the polished glass of the door, they saw his smile grow wider and then he was outside and away.Zeb stood in a doorway and watched offices spill people out, clutching briefcases and bags as they rushed to the nearest Metro station and head home.

He stood immobile for an hour, ignoring the indifferent looks of passersby. A security guard came and made to move him along, saw something in him and backed down.

The restaurant's doors swished open and Burke and Kowalski exited, glanced up and down briefly and flagged a cab. He saw Burke's head turn around and scan the street, and then her face grew small as the cab sped away.

She's good. Murphy was right.

But it won't hurt for me to make a few calls.Big G's eyes were narrow and angry as he stared at his underling.

'What do you mean, Parker wasn't Cezar?'

The underling shrank under his gaze and his words tumbled out.

Big G raised a hand. 'Stop.' The man stopped.

'Breathe.'

The man took a deep breath and spoke slower.Big G's men had put the word out on Zebadiah Carter but got no bites. The first name was uncommon and the gang had hoped someone would come forward, but no one did. They tried searching for Zeb Carter on the internet but hundreds of hits were returned. There was no way they could narrow down all of them.

A couple of men went back to their contact in the U.S. Marshal's office. The snitch swore he had given them the right details. Parker was Cezar. His computer said so.

The men believed him. The snitch had been held upside down from the top of a high rise. There was no reason for him to lie.

Big G's crew met in their favorite bar to see if collective wisdom could shed light on the subject. They passed pictures of Cezar and his woman around.

They shared Parker's photographs. Alcohol was consumed and jokes were cracked.

No progress was made.

A late entrant, Knuckles, pushed through the crowd, grabbed a drink and flipped through the photographs.

He frowned. 'This ain't her.'

No one heard him.

He withdrew his handgun and thumped its grip on the bar. It went silent.

'This ain't her. His bitch looked different.'

They stared at him as if he was crazy. 'Don't look at me like that,' Knuckles protested. 'Here, check her out yourself.'

He dragged out his cell phone, flicked through several photographs and pointed to one.

It was of Knuckles and Cezar, back in the day, but it was the third person that Knuckles was pointing at.

'Lookit her hair, her eyes, her nose. She's similar, but all you dumbasses missed one thing.'

He waited for the penny to drop and when it didn't, he rolled his eyes. 'Cezar's woman is taller, by at least half a foot.'

Big G's crew pored over the photographs and one by one, they sheepishly handed them back to Knuckles.

Knuckles was right. Cezar's woman was taller than Parker's woman.

Loud chatter broke out. Parker wasn't Cezar. But dang, didn't they look alike? They could be twins.

The couple of men went back to the snitch and this time they broke a finger.

The snitch squealed and said the details he gave were correct. He couldn't help it if the computer had the wrong details.

He could prove it.

They met him the next day and he showed them a printout from his computer.

It showed Cezar was Herb Parker, living at the address in Damascus.

'This is clearly shit. You got a junk address in your system.'

'That's what I said yesterday,' the snitch cried.'So we killed the wrong man?' Big G said slowly.

The underling nodded, his insides knotting in fear.

Just the week before, Big G had kneed a gang member in the groin. That dude wouldn't have kids. Ever again.

Big G thought about it, how it could have happened. The killing of an innocent didn't bother him.

His gang could have killed fifty more innocents and that still wouldn't have bothered him.

Maybe the Marshals used a dummy name and address without knowing such a real person existed.

He pushed the thought away from his mind. It wasn't important. Tracking Cezar and the stolen money, was.

'This Zeb Carter?'

'Boiler thinks Parker threw out a random name.'

Big G nodded slowly. He had seen it happen. People babbled whatever you wanted to hear when you were killing them slowly.

'So we're back to zero?'

The underling shuffled his feet.

'Boiler thinks we should track down men in small towns on the east coast. Who came there seven years back, have families similar in age to Cezar's. Small towns because that's what the Marshal's snitch said. They placed Cezar in a very small town. Boiler said chances are high he will still be in some small town. He won't break cover.'

The underling drew breath. Maybe it would be the last one he would draw if Big G didn't like what he had uttered.

Big G mulled it over in his mind and relaxed when the reasoning made sense. Boiler was thinking on the right lines. He spotted something in the underling.

'What else?'

'Boiler thought a man in New Jersey might be Cezar. Turned out, he wasn't. The man died.'

Big G shrugged. People died whenever they came in his or Boiler's way. No big deal.

'Keep looking.'

The underling nodded rapidly, knowing the conversation was almost over and he could escape Big G's burning eyes.

He started to leave when Big G's voice stopped him.

'Have someone watch Parker's house.'

Hunting You

Chapter 5

Boiler listened when the news was relayed back to him in Miami by a complex network of couriers and information bearers.

He was in the bar the gang owned, in an upstairs office that previously had been a booth in which the bar's strippers could get closer to male patrons.

Boiler glanced at the door when the hood had finished relaying Big G's orders; that was sufficient incentive for the hood to leave.

Not many of the gang were comfortable in Boiler's presence.

He was lean and tall, and his pale complexion made him look taller than his actual height, which was just a couple of inches over six feet.

He was bald; his green eyes glittered like marbles whenever they rested on an object or person of interest.

A scar on his left cheek, left by a knife wound, hadn't healed well and twitched whenever Boiler was angry. Or in the act of killing.

Boiler was seldom angry, however. He had an icy calmness around him that went very well with his catlike movements.

None of the gang members knew where he was from.

He never volunteered information, and the hoods didn't dare to ask him.

They all agreed that he was one big badass who was an asset to the gang. He was the second in command and ran the gang efficiently and ruthlessly in Big G's absence.

He was the only one who didn't sport the G tat. He didn't need to. Everyone in the criminal world knew who Boiler was and which gang he belonged to.Big G had found Boiler, bleeding and close to dying in Miami, when the two were teenagers.

Big G, then, ran a street gang that stole parts from the cars parked on the street.

He also ran a small amount of drugs, but those weren't his main business at that time. Boiler had been propped against a car's wheel, his face cut, his stomach slashed.

Big G dragged him upright, ignored the hiss of breath from the wounded youth and half carried, half dragged him, a couple of blocks away to his crib.

His crew surrounded him and the parade wound its way

slowly through wet, slippery pavements, past corners, and under streetlights.

In his crib, Big G stripped the shirt off the wounded youth, washed him, applied whatever little medical knowledge he had and left him alone.

Boiler took two weeks to recover; days during which Big G wondered at himself. He didn't have a sentimental bone in his body and he wondered what had prompted the impulsive action.

On the fifteenth day, Boiler uttered his first word.

'Karel,' he said, holding out a hand.

Big G took it, but was flummoxed. He didn't remember his birth name. He had grown up on the streets of the city.

He grinned through dirty teeth and shook Karel's hand. 'Big G.'

Over the days, Karel revealed a little of his story.

He was Ukrainian, had smuggled himself in a container ship from Odessa to Miami, when the heat in his native city had become unbearable.

He ran a few girls in Odessa and had added blackmail to his repertoire of services very recently.

He had picked the wrong man to threaten, a rival thug, head of a gang bigger and more powerful than Karel's.

That rival hood had ordered a hit on Karel, forcing him to flee the city.

In Miami, Karel had gotten into a knife fight with muggers and they had left him for dead.

Big G saw something in Karel's eyes and offered him sanctuary in his gang.

Karel killed his first man in his new home country, a couple of months later.

One of Big G's hoods was stealing from the take on the street and had to be punished. Big G thought of shooting him dead, but Karel had a better idea.

The Ukrainian had some thugs bring an enormous vat, had them fill it with oil and when the liquid reached its boiling point, he turned silently to the bound hood, lifted him easily and threw him into the oil.

Without uttering a single word.

The gang gave him the name, Boiler.

It suited him to a T.

Boiler brought a silent viciousness to the gang; every killing

44

or hit had to be ruthless, graphic and had to convey a message – Big G and his crew were not to be messed with.

With Big G's permission, he recruited gangbangers himself.

All similar to him, tall, heavy men who walked with a silent tread.

No one questioned Boiler's ascension in the gang but to avoid disharmony, Big G created an inner sanctum, a council, in which the heads of his various chapters, were members.

This inner sanctum rang the daily operations of the gang, with Boiler and Big G's oversight.

Big G brought a different style of management to running his gang.

Extreme ruthlessness where needed, but also profit sharing. Each chapter head was allowed to take home an agreed percentage of the monthly profits with a caveat – those profits had to be shared with the chapter members.

The gang's reputation spread and street thugs beat a line to Big G's door to join him.

Just before Big G had to flee to Mexico, his gang was a mix of ethnicities. East Europeans, Hispanics, a few Chinese and Blacks and Caucasians.

His gang's annual profit was in eight figures.

'No different than them fancy global corporations,' Big G often used to say.

Big G and Boiler brought not just a different management style but also a different operating style.

They used outsourcing.

Any hit that was contracted to the gang went through a qualification criterion.

If the hit had to be graphic, then the gang members, Boiler primarily, executed it themselves. If the hit had to be low key, the gang outsourced it to trusted contractors.

The Parker murders had been outsourced to such contractors, a bunch of three East European assassins based in Chicago.

Big G's gang didn't have anyone in the vicinity of Damascus and Boiler was occupied with carrying out another hit, so he couldn't go to that city. It made sense to use the contract killers.

Big G and Boiler had used them several times before and knew the men would do a professional job.

There were two advantages to using the assassins in tracking down Cezar. They helped the gang distance themselves from the hunt; let them focus on running their business.

The second advantage was that the assassins didn't rat. Even if they were caught.

They had even extended an offer to the assassins to join their gang. The assassins had declined. They valued their independence.

It was a code unique to them and in return, they charged extortionate fees. Fees that Big G and Boiler were glad to pay.

There was a third advantage that only Boiler and Big G were privy to. The assassins had a hacker in Ukraine who could work miracles and extract data from many secure sites.

Unfortunately, the U.S. Marshal's system was one the hacker hadn't been able to get into and hence the gang had to cultivate the snitch in that organization.

The Parker killings had been unique. They were meant to be low key, but given that Cezar/Parker wouldn't spill his secrets readily, the killings had become graphic.

Boiler and Big G had known that risk.Boiler met Ajdan, the leader of the assassins, in a café in Chicago that was filled with Big G's men.

Ajdan looked like any other person; there was nothing special about him. Black hair, black eyes, dressed in a dark shirt and jeans. He wouldn't stay in anyone's memory.

Boiler passed Big G's regards, Ajdan nodded in acknowledgement. Boiler updated Ajdan on what they knew.

That Parker was a false trail. That the name he had thrown out was a waste of time.

He updated Ajdan on the cops' progress on the investigation.

Over the years the gang had cultivated snitches in police departments of the cities they operated in and they had a good information flow.

'FBI has taken over. They have nothing.'

Ajdan swallowed a mouthful of black tea and said nothing. The FBI wouldn't have anything. He and his men were that good.

Boiler gave his shopping list to Ajdan. He needed a list of men, with families, who had come to small towns on the East Coast in the last seven years.

'Why?'

Boiler told him.

Ajdan stared at him. 'That's a lot of ground. Could be

millions of people.'

'Not necessarily. They have to be homeowners.' The Marshals would have set Cezar up with his own home. 'We know how Cezar and the woman look. We are looking at specific age groups.'

Ajdan looked thoughtful. That narrowed it down, but not by much. Cezar and his woman had average looks and seven years was a long time. People aged, wrinkled, lost hair.

'The towns should have no less than a hundred people and no more than a thousand.'

Ajdan looked askance at Boiler.

Boiler shrugged and repeated what the snitch had told them.

Small towns of those sizes had strong communities in which Cezar would blend in; their sizes acted like radar. Strangers were noted and watched. The Marshals had placed Cezar in such a town.

'He would be anonymous in larger cities.'

Boiler's smile was more of a grimace. Children cried when he smiled. 'We are active in large cities. We work with other gangs. We would have found him.'

'He could go to the west coast.'

'He didn't like it. His woman loved the east coast.'

'Did they have families? You could ask them?'

'We did.' The grimace came on again. A girl on a nearby table looked away quickly. 'They didn't know.'

Town council records, property records, driving licenses, passports. Ajdan ran the databases in his mind. His man could hack them. He had hacked some of them previously.

'It'll cost.'

'You'll get it.' Boiler said indifferently. 'Parker's home needs to be watched.'

'Why?'

'Someone might come visiting the Parker home. Someone who might know Cezar. We don't know how Parker got swapped for Cezar.'

'I can put someone there. He won't know why, or who he's working for.'

Boiler liked that. It was one reason Big G and he used the assassins. Their work was compartmentalized. One box might get opened, but it wouldn't lead to another.

They left separately. Ajdan first. A couple of Big G's hoods fell in behind him discreetly. They would make sure Ajdan wasn't tailed by anyone.

Boiler rose, glanced at the family at the nearby table and grimaced in politeness.

Just because he was a killer didn't mean he didn't have social graces.Back in his apartment in Jackson Heights, Zeb commanded Werner to dig out everything on Hank Parker.

Werner, housed in a supercomputer on Columbus Avenue in New York, could perform such searches in its sleep.

It didn't sleep of course. That was for humans.

It sent back a file to Zeb and his printer spat out neatly printed sheets.

The file didn't add much more to Zeb's knowledge of his mentor that he wasn't aware of.

After leaving the army, Hank, then in his late forties, had moved to Damascus with Emily and Cody. Petals had been born in Damascus.

Hank had used their savings to buy out a family run home repair business and had grown that into a thriving business that employed twenty people.

He built small homes, erected greenhouses, garden sheds, and small offices. He sometimes landscaped gardens and built swimming pools.

Zeb asked Werner to look into Hank's and Emily's finances. They were clean. They would be. Hank had his code.

His fingers tightened on the sheets of paper. He consciously relaxed them, dropped the sheets on his desk and wandered to a window.

An ambulance raced by, its wail coming to him dimly through thick sheets of glass. Its lights cast red and blue shadows in his living room and then they died.

He went to his kitchen, opened shelves, heated water, and spooned coffee. The first sip went deep inside and steadied him.

He returned to the papers. He got Werner to search for Hank's business associates and his employees for anything out of the ordinary. There wasn't.

He went online and checked out their social media profiles. Hank didn't have one, but Emily had an active one, going by the comments and posts on her pages.

He asked Werner to look into all those who had posted on her pages. Werner came back a few minutes later, reported nothing suspicious about them.

Was either of them having an affair?

Nope. That didn't feel like a revenge killing. He brought the photographs of the killing in his mind and examined them.

Someone wanted information.

What did Hank know? Did they get it?

He looked out of the window. *Not yet dark.* He calculated distances and times in his mind.

I can sleep in my ride.Damascus was close to six hundred miles from his apartment. Zeb went to the basement parking lot and pressed a button on his key fob and heard a satisfying growl from the cavernous interior.

A Suburban's lights guided him to the vehicle and the door closed after him with a satisfyingly heavy thump.

It would. The vehicle was armored with sheets of steel and could stop all but tank shells.

Its interior bristled with equipment that didn't come from the dealer. Under its hood were a couple hundred more horses than the manufacturer had built.

An hour later, Zeb was free from the long reaching grasp of the city.

He skirted Philadelphia, and entered Maryland, by then it was dark and the universe had fallen silent. The soft radio in his ride carried him relentlessly over the ribbon of road, concrete that flowed like a smooth river beneath his wheels. He stopped once at a rest area and the solitariness of the land reminded him of Libya.

I hope Omar and Abdul are fine.

After killing Umkhayey, Zeb had returned to where the herders were still sleeping off the drugs in their system.

He had bundled them in the terrorists' vehicle and driven them to Taknis where he left them with their pockets bulging with currency.

I couldn't leave them on the plains. Umkhayey's men would have suspected them and wiped them out.

A truck roared past, its wash rocking his SUV and blowing away the tendrils of the past.

He gassed the vehicle and continued his drive past Martinsburg and Winchester and when exhaustion was creeping up on him, he drove through the town of Harrisonburg, named after an early settler, Thomas Harrison.

He drove through the dozing streets and sleepy lights till he found a secluded parking space and stretched back and went to sleep.

He pushed on before dawn and reached Damascus just before ten.

He checked into a motel, freshened himself and drove around the town to get his bearings.

The town had a population of less than a thousand but received several hundred visitors a year due to its location in the Blue Mountains and its promise of an outdoors experience.

Zeb entered a diner on Main Street, dodged a backpacking couple and seated himself next to a large window through which sunlight streamed and bathed the eatery in a golden glow.

He ate leisurely, watching the world pass by; backpackers, cyclists, families - the town attracted all kinds of visitors.

The waitress bustled across, refilled his cup, attempted to make small talk and drifted away at his polite smile and lack of response.

Hank's home was two streets to the north of Main Street, on the east side of Laurel Creek which wended through the town.

Zeb drove through the near empty street, noted the large homes set back from sidewalks, and finally spotted the large white house in front of which there was a flagpole, with a flag fluttering in the light breeze.

Zeb scanned ahead and behind; a few cars parked on the street, a few more on driveways of a few homes.

He parked in front of a house that bore a 'For Sale' sign and walked to the Parker residence.

Ribbons of yellow tape still partly surrounded the house. He ducked under the tape and circled the house casually, taking photographs on his phone.

From behind the cover of the trunk of a tree, he surveyed the surroundings. The nearest neighbor was to his right, several hundreds of yards away, separated by a lush lawn, green undergrowth, and several trees. The street was visible and so were a few cars.

No one came out to watch him. He was too far to notice if any curtains twitched. He shrugged mentally and went to the back of the house, tried the back door and found it locked.

He walked on, found a locked kitchen window that yielded to the sharp blade of his knife and swung open easily.

He stepped inside and the smell of unmaintained house came to him. It was quiet; there was not even the click or hum of appliances.

He walked through the large kitchen that could seat ten, through a hallway that branched out into a games room, a couple of bedrooms, a bathroom, and then opened into the living room.

Couches and rugs dotted the living room, a mantelpiece brimmed with photographs and trophies.

Shooting trophies, family pictures, baby pictures, Hank in uniform, Hank and Emily with their arms around each other, Hank tossing young Cody in the air.

At the back, almost hidden behind family pictures, Zeb found one picture of Hank with his unit.

There were ten men in the photograph, all of them uniformed, cradling their guns casually, all smiling.

They were young and had the air of invincibility that youth carried. They had lost that look soon and only some of them were alive now.

His eyes didn't linger on a brown-haired young man at the back who was smiling widely at the camera. That smile didn't exist anymore.

He extracted the photograph and slipped it inside his jacket.

The living room opened into an equally large dining room. He didn't look in its direction. He went up the stairs and surveyed more bedrooms and bathrooms, looked out the windows and saw a large back yard in which a swing hung motionless.

An inflated pool lay in a corner, its surface covered by leaves and branches and dead insects.

He went to the largest bedroom and started searching.

Three hours later he had nothing. In the movies, the cops always found clues. There was always an 'ah-ha moment,' though no one said that anymore.

There was no such moment in Hank's home.

There were papers, diaries, journals, bank statements, computers, invoices, bills, letters, but not one of them conveyed any threat to Hank or his family.

Zeb searched the other bedrooms but knew he was lingering, postponing. He went to the landing, took a breath and walked down to the living room and then to the dining room.

The dining table could seat eight and was laid out neatly

with the chairs tucked in deep, napkins and cutlery arranged in the center.

The air hung thick and heavy and he thought he detected the familiar coppery smell. *It's my imagination. The killings were more than four months back.*

The floor was dark hardwood and felt like oak when he ran his fingers over it. He went to the head of the table that faced the living room, rested his arms lightly on the chair and pictured it.

Hank, at the head of the table, Cody and Petals next to him, Emily at the end.

He would have ladled food in their plates, cracked jokes, laughed loudly, kissed the tops of their heads. Just another night in the Parker family.

Except it wasn't.

He bent down finally and ran his eyes along the floor. The traces of blood were impossible to detect since the house had been cleaned professionally.

Hank and Emily had no surviving family on either side; however, their family lawyer had arranged for the home to be cleaned and was now dealing with their estate.

He closed his eyes and brought up the crime scene pictures in his mind. He went to the spots where the blood splotches would have been. The hardwood floor gleamed back at him.

He pushed the table to one end, arranged the chairs in the center and sat in the central one.

They made Hank watch. Just like I was made to…

He closed his eyes tightly and willed the thought and the accompanying images to disappear.

Back into the white box in his mind, which would slam back into rows and rows of white boxes, indistinguishable from one another.

The thought refused, the images resisted. They had been denied for so long, they wanted to escape.

No. You can't.

Alone in the empty home where his friend and his family had been murdered, Zeb summoned the fog to come rescue him, drown him in its welcoming greyness.

It roiled and approached reluctantly.

He recalled the breathing exercise he had been taught by old men in far corners of the world.

He stood there for several minutes, unmoving, till the fog

cleared his mind, disappeared slowly, till his breathing slowed and his pulse returned to normal.

He unclenched his fists and detected the slightest tremble in his fingers. He wiped his forehead. His palms came away damp.

He went to the kitchen, drew water from the tap and drank steadily till the cold liquid filled him and brought back the man the world knew.

He went back to the dining room, rearranged the table and when he pushed the chairs in place, something sharp poked his chest.

He felt inside his jacket and fingered the sharp edges of the photograph he had pocketed.

I've got your back, boy. Hank, from a million years away, from a distant land.

The beast came to life, filled him and turned his eyes bleak.

They're dead, Hank. They don't know it yet.

Hunting You

Chapter 6

Maximus yawned lustily, scrunched lower in his car, glanced once at the feed on his car's dashboard, saw nothing that was of interest and yawned again.

Maximus had spotted the dude the moment the dull black SUV entered the Parker's street.

Damascus had pickup trucks, sedans, SUVs, vehicles of all kinds, but after hanging around in the town for a week, Maximus recognized most of the neighborhood residents' rides. The tourists – they didn't visit this part of town. The restaurants and hotels were closer to Main Street.

Maximus was a gifted lifter, a pickpocket, who made his living by relieving men and women – he was an equal opportunity thief – of their wallets and purses.

He was proud of his skill. He has a way of getting close to his marks, sometimes befriending them, without their ever suspecting him.

He could fade into the scenery if he wished to. He became furniture and didn't rate a first glance, let alone a second one.

His light brown skin and average features rendered him anonymous. His clothing and gait made him invisible. He could dress like a stockbroker if needed, or sprawl on the sidewalk like a drunk if that was what it took.

One time he had dined on the same table as his mark, a big time hood in Chicago, had laughed at his crude jokes and had snapped several photographs of the mark on his phone.

He had grown up in Fuller Park, had fallen in with a gang who stole cars, mugged passersby and broke into properties.

Maximus was smarter than his buddies, realized it was just a short hop away from bigger and more violent crimes. He wanted none of that.

He had discovered a long time back that he had light fingers; he broke away from the gang and pursued a solo career as a lifter.

It had paid off handsomely. He had his own pad, his own wheels, a bright yellow Mustang which was a babe magnet; it was the best investment he had made.

Life was going well for Maximus, till he lifted from the wrong guy.

The wrong guy turned out to be the most powerful hood in Chicago, a lean, mean, ebony-skinned man who trapped

Maximus's straying hand with ease, looked at him with lizard eyes and dragged him to a bar.

He threw the lifter's ass in a seat, clicked his fingers and a knife was produced by his goons. He grabbed Maximus's hand and brought the knife down without a word.

The lifter closed his eyes and screamed, opened them dazedly when he heard chuckles and looked down to see the knife buried millimeters from his fingers.

'Who are you?' Lizard Eyes rasped.

Maximus spilled out everything, and when he had finished, silence fell in the bar.

Lizard Eyes looked back at his hand as if tempted to sever it from his body, but when he raised those coal grey eyes, he had a proposition for Maximus.

Maximus would take contracts from him. Maximus agreed. He would have agreed to anything. He had a fond attachment to his extremities and any proposition that meant they stayed attached was a good one.

The contracts came. A businessman's briefcase, a lawyer's bag, a cop's files. Sometimes the work was just shadowing a mark and recording his movements. The money was great. Life was good. Maximus was on top of the world. Damascus was one such contract from Lizard Eyes. It was an easy one. All that Maximus had to do was keep watch on a house, record whoever came to the house, follow any such person and report back to Lizard Eyes. Simple. No hassle.

Maximus rented an inconspicuous Ford for his watch, parked himself on the street just up from the house and kept watch.

Nothing happened for three days and then the dude turned up in the SUV.

Maximus had rigged his phone to feed into the Ford's display console; he had duct taped the phone to the window.

The phone looked out and fed to the display. Maximus pushed his seat back, brought a newspaper to his face, punched a hole through it and watched the display.

Hands free surveillance. Risk free surveillance. It was money in the bank.

Till it wasn't.The dude had disappeared inside the house, hours ago. There was no sign of him, no shadow crossed the window.

Maximus stifled a yawn and made to settle more comfortably, when he froze.

The passenger door opened and the dude slipped in smoothly, as if he was made of liquid.

The dude turned his head toward Maximus and brown eyes rested on him.

Lizard Eyes made Maximus's skin crawl.

This dude's look made it want to separate itself from his body and flee.Zeb had spotted the Ford on his second pass on the street. It was parked between a pickup truck and a minivan and had a good sightline to the Parker home.

He hadn't given it any thought initially, but the faint movement from inside it had snagged his attention.

Damascus wasn't a town where folks idled in their cars. Residents had jobs to go to, visitors had places to go.

He had driven past, and from the shadows of an upper bedroom, he had extracted a cable camera – a tubular device with a lens at one end and phone jack at the other – and had observed the Ford.

Watching the house. Black or brown-skinned man, young. Short hair, clean shaven, neatly dressed. Pretending to read a newspaper. Not looking at the house. Decent tradecraft.

However, people don't hang about in cars in this town.

He had exited the house from the rear, run across the green to the neighboring house, climbed over their fence, and had come up from behind the Ford. He then used the pickup truck as cover and silently slid into the watcher's car.

He ignored the startled squawk from the watcher, ran his eyes swiftly over his body and saw no weapons on him. The watcher's hands were visible and empty.

'Who are you?'

The watcher didn't respond. His eyes were wide, his mouth gaped open.

Zeb removed his Glock from his shoulder holster and placed it on the wide armrest between them.

'This is the hard way. You know the easy one.'Maximus spilled. Words came out of him like a river bursting at the banks. Sweat beaded his face and ran down his cheeks, Maximus ignored it. Staying alive was more important. He watched the dude's face for any response.

There wasn't. It seemed to be made of granite.

'You don't know why this guy wanted me followed?'

'No, sir, I swear– '

The dude cut him off with a wave of the gun.

Maximus stifled a moan. First Lizard Eyes, now this dude.

He tried to control his breathing and bladder, sat silently and watched the dude. The dude didn't look back. He was staring straight ahead, seemingly lost in thought.

Minutes passed, seemed like hours, and whatever little hope Maximus had, started bleeding away. He opened his mouth to plead one last time, shut it with a click when the dude lifted a finger without looking in his direction.

How in hell did he know I was going to speak?

The dude sat like that Buddha guy for another fifteen minutes and all the while Maximus's phone fed a stream, now pointless, from the house to the display.

'Aristo Churchey? That's his name?'

Maximus bobbed his head. That was Lizard Eyes.

'Who's he?'

Maximus's eyes grew round. Who hadn't heard of Aristo?

'Dude, he runs Chicago. Nothing happens in that town that he doesn't have a hand in. You want some smack, paradise, roach, whatever makes you high - Aristo supplies it. You want babes, he has the best ones in town. You want your man in the City Council? Aristo will arrange it.'

His voice dropped. 'You want a rival to disappear? He can do that for you.'

The brown eyes swung toward him. 'The cops don't know about him?'

Maximus snorted. 'Sure, they do. But without that evidence thing, there ain't much they can do. Way I heard it, even the Commissioner is in his pocket.'

'Superintendent.'

'What?'

'They have a police superintendent, not a commissioner.'

Maximus shrugged the titles away. 'Whatever. Street talk is that Aristo owns that dude.'

'I want to meet him.'

'The cop guy?' Maximus asked stupidly.

'Aristo.'

'You got a death wish, man?' Maximus yelled. 'I'm a goner.

You'll plug me and throw me in some river, but why do you want to die?'

'I won't kill you.'

The words took a while to sink into Maximus.

'You won't?' He asked slowly, hardly believing what he had heard.

'No.'

Maximus closed his eyes and thanked the Lord, thanked the dude, thanked his momma and poppa and grabbed the dude's hand, his free hand, and shook it.

Air hadn't felt sweeter; the universe hadn't felt more colorful. That babe waiting for him was in for a torrid time.

He felt the weight of the brown eyes on him and his euphoria receded. 'What about all this?' He gestured at the feed in the display unit.

'What was the plan?'

'I was to report back to Aristo, send him your pictures and videos.'

'Stick to your plan.'

Maximus gave him incredulous. 'He'll know about you then, won't he?'

The dude didn't reply.

'He'll kill you if you approach him. He'll know you're in town the moment you are in Chicago.'

'Will he?'

The dude's face didn't change, but Maximus got the impression he was smiling. The man glanced at him one last time, slid out of the Ford and walked away without a backward glance.

Once Maximus had clicked his mouth shut, he called out of the window. 'Who're you, man? Do you have a name?'

The dude didn't reply, didn't look back, as he walked back to his SUV.

Maximus continued watching him; the way he moved brought to his mind a TV program he had watched a while back.

A cheetah had stalked a deer in the African wild, creeping slowly through the grass, almost invisible amongst it, barely ruffling the stalks, and then had burst into glorious speed.

For some reason the dude reminded Maximus of that animal.

He watched till the man disappeared inside the SUV, its tail lights flared and the vehicle disappeared.

Maximus powered up his ride and couldn't resist a grin.

'Aristo baby, you'd better tuck that tail between your hind legs and run as hard and fast as you can.' Zeb turned on his laptop, connected it to the vehicle's WiFi and opened a voice command window to Werner.

'Maximus,' he spelt the name as he navigated out of Damascus and floored it once he hit the US-58. Chicago was ten hours away if he drove non-stop.

An electronic voice interrupted his thinking.

'Be precise. Which Maximus do you want? Roman generals, Authors, Bishops, fiction characters?'

Zeb stared at his laptop for a second.

He could have sworn the metallic voice had a trace of irony in it. He imagined Beth and Meghan high-fiving each other and snickering. He wouldn't put it past them to program Werner to respond in that manner.

'Maximus, Chicago. Pick pocket. Thief. Gangbanger.'

'You should've said so in the first place.'

The twins *had* played around with the software program.

The program spoke to him a few seconds later, reciting the lifter's rap sheet. He hadn't done time; he had been arrested a couple of times but had been let off each time due to lack of evidence. For the last few years, he hadn't fallen afoul of the law.

He is good.

He commanded Werner to dig out intel on Aristo Churchey and what came back filled more than an hour of his drive.

The gangster had a hand in every conceivable criminal activity in Chicago and while he had been questioned several times by the cops, he had been released every time.

Good lawyers and good organization.

Churchey presented himself as a construction baron and built low cost housing for the poor. He ran a hospital and several private schools. He donated large sums to charity and yet the links to crime didn't disappear.

Werner recited a long list of killings that Churchey was alleged to have ordered.

A reporter who was investigating him, a couple of cops, a DEA agent, several politicians, other gangbangers.

'Approach him with care.' The program told him.

A smile tugged Zeb's lips and disappeared swiftly.

I just want some answers.

Hunting You

Chapter 7

'You got nothing else?' Churchey sifted through the photographs Maximus had printed and then turned his cold eyes on the lifter.

'No, sir. I couldn't get close enough to him to pick his wallet.' Maximus knew the gang boss liked the *Sir*, though he never showed it.

'He just went inside the house, came out and drove away?'

'Yes, sir.'

Maximus was in Churchey's mansion, surrounded by gun toting goons.

He could see a swimming pool through the glass doors; several women frolicking in it. He felt the gangster's eyes on him and he dragged his gaze back.

'You seem different.'

Maximus controlled the surge of fear in him and put on his game face. 'Just tired. It was a long drive and I haven't slept well.'

Churchey pinned him down for a few more seconds, nodded, and rose. Two goons stepped forward and escorted him out and watched him till he drove away.

Maximus wiped the sweat on his palms against his thigh once he was clear of the mansion and the tightly wound spring in him began to relax. He was expecting to be plugged the moment Churchey pinned those eyes on him.

'I gotta get one of them PhDs in lying. I didn't know I was that good,' he mumbled and grinned widely and winked at a blonde in a red convertible.

Hot dang. Life was good. That was twice he'd come close to being killed and he'd walked away both times.

'I wonder what that dude's up to?'Churchey looked at the pictures one last time, threw them on the table and stretched and yawned.

A buxom girl came to him and brought him a drink. He slapped her on her ass, watched it jiggle while he considered his next actions.

The dude wasn't of interest to him. He had been paid to have him followed and Maximus had delivered.

Churchey was interested in maximizing his profit, but first he had to know how badly the East Europeans wanted this dude.

He snapped his fingers and the girl brought a cell phone. He recited a number and she punched it and held the phone against his ear.

Aristo Churchey didn't hold phones, didn't dial them. He had people who did that.

A guttural voice came on when the phone had rung three times. 'Yeah?'

'I got him.' 'Who is he?' Ajdan asked Churchey after skimming through the pictures and the video.

Churchey shrugged his shoulders. The East Europeans had subcontracted the trace to Churchey and he had delivered. The 'who,' and 'why,' of the dude didn't matter to him.

Ajdan looked at the man in the pictures again, but it wasn't anyone he had come across before.

Ajdan and his buddies had operated in Kosovo and Serbia, as well as a few other Balkan states. When they relocated to the States, they had hooked up with Boiler and Big G, along with a few other gangs.

They were choosy about their kills and steered clear of cop killing.

'Could he be a cop?'

Churchey glanced at the pictures again and shook his head. 'Doesn't look like one. He's not from the Chicago P.D. for sure. I checked. In any case, a cop wouldn't drive around in that SUV. Those wheels don't come cheap.'Boiler frowned, his thick eyebrows forming a bridge across his forehead. 'Who the hell is he?'

He was still in Chicago, attending to business. Product needed to be sold, women needed to be brought in and put to work in their 'houses.'

Ajdan shrugged. He didn't know. They were in the same café they had met, with the same large men hanging about.

'Can you find out?'

'With just a photograph to go on?' Ajdan considered. 'Can't be done unless the dude is a well-known person.'

'You have the SUV's plates.'

Boiler flipped through the pictures and held one up that showed the numerals clearly.

'That'll help.' Ajdan pocketed the picture. 'Why can't you

find out yourself? You've got contacts in the DMV.'

Boiler shook his head. 'Big G doesn't want our footprints on this.'

Ajdan didn't reply, instead brought out a list from a pocket. A list that made Boiler's eyes gleam.

'How many names?'

'Fifteen. All of them fit the profile.'

Boiler gripped his shoulder hard and left without a word. Now he could go hunting.'It isn't Cezar?' Big G surveyed the underling in front of him.

The underling shook his head. He was new; the previous guy had his jaw broken by Big G.

'So why's he at the Parker place?'

The underling wisely didn't answer. He had been told speaking less was a good way to surviving long, around Big G.

The gang boss flexed his massive shoulders and popped his knuckles as he paced his small cell.

Why would anyone visit the Parker home after so long? Any friends he had, would have been done visiting by now.

'Boiler is finding out?'

The underling nodded.

Big G relaxed. Boiler would find out.

A flick of his fingers and the underling scurried away. Big G lay on his bunk and dreamed red. Dreams filled with images of Cezar, his body mutilated by Boiler.Churchey spent the day running his business, taking a contract to kill a nosey politician and bribing a few cops.

He inspected a new batch of girls and supervised the renovation of a nightclub. He met a few Cubans and negotiated a large crack deal and when it was eight p.m., headed back to the mansion.

The guard hurried across to his limo and when he saw Churchey, his head bobbed and he opened the gates.

The previous guard had let in Churchey's limo without verifying the passengers. His body was now rotting in a landfill site.

A flunky brought Churchey a glass of water, another brought him a freshly-laundered towel and a third took his cell phone.

Churchey climbed the stairs, undressed, tossed his clothes on the bed and headed to the Jacuzzi in the bathroom.

It had been set to the desired temperature, a change of clothes was neatly arranged on a hanger, fluffy towels and a bathrobe hung nearby.

Churchey lowered his body, laid back with a sigh and reached out for a glass of wine. The first sip went down like a slow fire and he closed his eyes. All that killing, bribing, dealing led to this.

He idly considered which woman would share his bed that night when a draught of cool air blew over him.

He opened his eyes and the wine glass slipped in the water.

'Who the fuck are you?' He shouted at the man in front of him. He yelled loudly for his guards.

No footsteps came pounding, the bathroom door stubbornly stayed shut. He shouted again, controlled the flicker of fear in him. No reply from outside.

The brown-haired man watched him in silence; his quiet manner enraged Churchey and he gripped the sides of the Jacuzzi to raise himself.

The stranger knocked his hands away, Churchey fell back in the water with a splash.

Churchey had crawled up the gang ladder in Chicago. Some dude wasn't going to get the better of him.

Dude?

A cold chill raced through him when he recognized the stranger from Maximus's pictures.

His hand darted to a panel in the sidewall, beneath which lay a handgun, spare magazines, and a hunting knife.

His hand didn't reach the wall, it was lazily slapped away.

He drove his body forward with a guttural curse, to ram his head in the stranger's middle and crush him in a bear hug.

His ears rang when another lazy slap struck him on the face. He fell back in the water, but he wasn't done. He surged upward suddenly, reaching out for the dude.

The stranger waited till the last second and instead of ducking away from the blow, grabbed Churchey's hands, dragged him out of the bath and dumped him on the floor.

Churchey dove at his legs, fell back when a knee caught him in the face.

His nose burst, blood streamed down his cheeks, over his chest, formed dark round shapes on the polished floor.

Churchey stared at the drops for a second. He couldn't recall when he had last shed blood.

The thought brought a red mist down; he uncoiled his body and struck faster than a snake, aiming at the stranger's groin.

His hand met empty air, the next moment it was caught in a steel grip, twisted, turned so far back that Churchey's tendons and joints screamed in agony.

He howled when something snapped and blacked out for a few seconds and when he came to, his body felt as if on fire.

He ran his eyes dully, rested them on his right arm which lay at an unnatural angle, moved them up with great effort to see the dude crouch beside him.

'What's your interest in me?'Boiler was with two hitters in Buckeystown, Maryland, two days later.

He had sifted through the photographs of the fifteen men, some of them with their women, had put aside five, compared the remaining with those of Cezar and his wife.

He thought the ten looked like a good match, given that he didn't have any recent pictures of the traitor. His men nodded in assent when he handed out the photographs. Yeah, those ten looked likely.

He read the dossiers of the ten men that Ajdan had provided. The time window was good, the backstories looked good.

He randomly picked one photograph, that of Dirk Beatty, catering business owner.

Dirk Beatty would have the privilege of being the first to meet Boiler.He picked his men and cut through Illinois, Ohio, Pennsylvania and entered Maryland.

They stopped in small towns for fueling up, ate in family run bars and restaurants, smiled politely at residents who looked their way, did their best to disguise the silent menace they exuded.

Buckeystown had less than a thousand residents, one gas station, several motels and eateries, most of which were scattered around the single road, Buckeystown Pike, that ran through the town.

Boiler stopped at the gas station, filled their tank and when he went inside to pay, a white-haired woman behind the counter smiled brightly at him and tried to make small talk.

Small talk wasn't Boiler's forte. He replied in a series of grunts and monosyllables.

Come far?

Grunt.

Going far?

Grunt.

Nice day for a drive.

Uh huh.

That's a nice SUV you have. Is it new?

For a second Boiler thought of shooting her; instead he gave her his trademark grimace and left quickly.

He had wanted to ask directions to the catering business, but her inquisitiveness put him off.

He hadn't noticed any CCTV cameras in the store and their SUV had local plates, but it was a small town.

It ran on gossip. He had already given her enough material to fill several hours.

He nodded at her wave as he drove off. The gas station was right on the Pike; he followed it for a mile and came to another crossroad, around which were a convenience store, a cafe of some kind, a garage, another store, a few homes and then signs of life thinned out.

Boiler was still thinking of the old woman and missed reading the signs on the various stores till a shout from the rear alerted him.

'It's right there,' one of his hitters yelled and pointed at the cafe that was receding in the distance.

Boiler looked ahead; there seemed to be a bend in the Pike. He went around it, checked for traffic, made a U-turn and headed back to the junction.

Buckey's Cakes and Catering was right on the junction, next to the convenience store.

It was a white-walled building that had a small seating area, had a few cars parked outside, and saw relatively high traffic for the area.

Dirk Beatty had a cafe attached to his catering business. Boiler thought about it for a while, figuring out the implications on what he was planning to do.

There were none. The cafe made sense. Small towns with populations similar to Buckeystown, wouldn't have enough demand for a catering business to stand on its own.

Their first problem became obvious. There was no place to conceal themselves, observe Beatty's business, and follow him.

Boiler turned around in his vehicle, surveyed the two men

with him, pointed silently at the one who looked the most presentable.

The hitter would enter Beatty's restaurant just before closing time, stay there, make small talk till Beatty closed and when he drove home, Boiler would make his move.

Their second problem became apparent when the hitter entered the restaurant. Beatty and his wife, Jane, had their home in the same building.

The upper story was their residence; the ground floor was the business.

Then they got lucky. The hitter said he lived in Frederick which was just six miles away but was interested in buying a home away from the city.

Buckeystown looked good to him on the map, that was enough for him to drive out and have a look. He liked what he had seen so far.

Dirk Beatty agreed with him and extolled the virtues of his hometown. He looked the hitter up and down. 'I'm heading to Frederick tomorrow, myself. I'm running low on sugar and flour, without which cakes ain't going to get baked here.'

He turned, greeted a customer, turned back to the hitter. 'Why don't you meet me here in the morning? I'll show you the best parts of this town in the daylight, before I leave for Frederick. Maybe that'll help you make a decision.'

The hitter was flummoxed momentarily; he wasn't used to small town hospitality. For a moment, he wondered if Beatty had made him, but the man's wide smile and warm eyes dispelled his fears.

He accepted Beatty's offer. They agreed on a time to meet, shook hands and the hitter left with a large slice of cake that Beatty thrust toward him.

Boiler listened silently to his download. 'You sure he didn't make you?'

'Yeah.' The hitter's voice came thickly through a mouthful of cake.

'Anyone hear you?'

The hitter shook his head.

Boiler turned the key and drove away, satisfied. Dirk Beatty had handed himself to them. The grab couldn't have been planned better. The grab was easy to execute the next day.

The hitter drove to Beatty's store at the agreed time to find the store owner and his wife waiting for him.

Beatty and the hitter greeted each other, introductions to the wife were made, Beatty made a *follow me* motion with his hand and climbed into a red pickup truck that had seen better days.

'It's her.' The hitter said breathlessly when he climbed into their SUV.

Boiler nodded, waited as the pickup coughed once, belched smoke, and trundled away.

He wasn't worried about Beatty or his wife recognizing the hitter. His men had joined the gang after Cezar's disappearance.

They drove away, just the two vehicles on the street, one carrying helpful neighbors, another carrying grim violence.

Boiler waited for a stretch of road that he'd noticed while driving in, about a hundred yards of asphalt lined with thick growth on either side.

He looked far ahead when they reached that stretch.

Other than the pickup truck ahead, there wasn't anything else to see. The ribbon they were on disappeared into blue sky in the distance.

He revved their SUV and rammed the truck from behind. Its rear buckled under the impact and it slid sideways.

Beatty tried to control it, but a second impact drove the pickup off the road, into the undergrowth.

Boiler saw Beatty trying to wrestle with the wheel, and then with the door.

He didn't give the store owner or his woman a chance to get out. He smashed into the vehicle again, pushed it deep through grass, bushes, and stunted trees, till the truck stalled and silence fell.

Boiler emerged swiftly from his SUV, didn't spare a glance at the front of his vehicle, motioned at his two men.

One of them went back to the road and sought cover. He would keep watch.

The other accompanied Boiler. They split when they approached the vehicle.

Boiler dragged the dazed Beatty out, the second hitter slapped his wife when she started screaming, grabbed her by the waist and threw her out. He slapped her again to subdue her, shoved her to the ground beside her husband.

They cuffed their captives' hands, slapping them occasionally to cow them into submission.

Beatty and his wife didn't offer much resistance. They were still in shock, which was compounded by the repeated blows rained on them.

Boiler paused before taping Beatty's mouth, looked into the man's eyes.

'Hello, Cezar, where's our money?'

Beatty's eyes stared blankly back at him. His wife struggled violently, shouted unintelligibly through the gag over her mouth. Her eyes were wide and Boiler thought he saw recognition in them.

He smiled slightly and brought out his blade.Beatty and his wife died three hours later.

Blood from their bodies had darkened the ground around them. The sky had heard their deep groans and had witnessed their thrashing. The sky didn't help.

Boiler removed his gloves, wiped his hands against his trousers, bit back the cold rage that threatened to drown him.

Beatty wasn't Cezar. His wife wasn't Cezar's woman.

He lost his control for a second, swore loudly, kicked at the dead man in his stomach, in the head, in the groin. His two hitters pulled him back, and started wrapping the couple in plastic sheets.

Boiler crouched beside the bodies, removed a couple of photographs from his jacket, compared them to the dead couple.

He shook his head bitterly. They looked the same, but in the three hours of knife work, Beatty had steadfastly maintained his story.

He wasn't Cezar. He didn't know who that was.

He rose, ice-cold control returning to him, gestured at his men to resume the wrapping.

They dug graves and buried the plastic-clad bodies in them, covered the graves and went back to the vehicles.

A hitter tried the pickup truck. Its engine turned reluctantly, but it turned. He threw it in reverse, backed it out carefully and drove to the road where he fell behind Boiler.

Late in the day, just inside Pennsylvania, when the sky was turning orange, Boiler set fire to the red truck in a dump yard that he had used before.

He watched the flames leap up and consume the vehicle.

They didn't consume his rage.

Where was Cezar?

Chapter 8

Big G grabbed at the underling, smashed his head against the wall in rage, made to smash it again when a couple of guards rushed in and separated them.

Beatty was not Cezar.

The underling's words rang in his mind long after lights had turned out in the prison. Big G lay in his solitary cell, stared up at nothing and figured out his moves.

He wasn't worried about the beatings the guards inflicted on him. He wasn't bothered about the solitary confinement. His money ensured that the guards went easier on him than most other prisoners. Hell, if he wanted, he could've escaped from the prison a long time back.

If that El Chapo guy could escape from his max-security prison, so could Big G. He did not have that Chapo guy's wealth and reach, but Big G was no mere prisoner either. The only reason he stayed put was the Feds. They wouldn't let up on the hunt, would make life unbearable for him if he escaped to the U.S.

It was better if he stayed in his Mexican prison till they forgot about him. It wasn't as if his empire was crumbling just because he was behind bars.

Nothing's lost.

Except for the thirty million.

His fists turned into huge knots till the tendons on his arms stood out like rubber pipes.

Boiler should keep hunting. No other choice. Maybe he should find that stranger too and question him.The stranger was in a café in Chicago, in an oasis of calm amidst the hustle of the city. He was aware of people coming, going, cups clinking, occasional laughter. None of those registered deeply.

He was going through pictures, photographs, names, in his memory.

Zeb was searching for Armenian assassins he had come across. In particular, he was seeking out one called Ajdan.

Churchey had sobbed through his pain as he revealed everything he knew.

Ajdan had contracted Churchey who in turn had set Maximus to follow Zeb. Churchey didn't know why the Armenian wanted Zeb followed and he hadn't asked. In

Churchey's world, money talked. Reasons didn't matter.

Churchey had met Ajdan just twice. The first time had been several years back when the two men had commenced their business alliance.

The second time was when Ajdan had come to collect Maximus's surveillance photographs of Zeb.

Churchey knew that the Ajdan was an assassin, and came with good references. The Armenian had carried out a few hits for him. Churchey, in turn, had occasionally ferreted out info for the assassin.

Their business was usually conducted remotely, through burner phones and dummy email accounts.

Churchey knew Ajdan had a couple of other killers working with him.

Zeb went through the countries he had been to, which covered large parts of a world map.

Nope. In all his years of hunting men, no one called Ajdan had crossed his path.

It could be an alias. Most probably it is.

He considered his options.

The twins, with their boyfriends, had joined Roger, Bwana, and their girlfriends and the eight of them were hiking and camping somewhere in Mexico's forests.

Bear and Chloe were in Nepal. Broker was still in New York, but Zeb knew he had hooked up with a new girlfriend.

Clare was in D.C. Vacations were alien to her. However, this wasn't an agency mission.

He shook his head unconsciously, missed the disappointed look a blonde cast his way.

My team deserves their downtime. I can do this myself.

He plugged his laptop into a socket, turned on his sat-phone giving him encrypted access to the internet, connected to Werner and typed in the search parameters.

Zeb could talk to the program with simple search terms. The twins or Broker took care of anything more complex.

He imagined Werner sniffing in disdain, if it could.

Armenian assassin named Ajdan. That's all you got?

Yeah. If you're the world's greatest super computer, prove it.

He shut down his computer, stowed it away, stilled, when a thought struck him.

Maximus. Churchey will take it out on Maximus.Maximus was living high for a few days.

Rumor was that Churchey had his face re-arranged. Maximus could guess who was behind that, if rumor was true.

However, Maximus hadn't lived to reach his late twenties without being cautious.

He knew there was a chance Aristo would be hunting for him and hence he took great care. He switched apartments, rented a new set of wheels, stopped lifting for a while.

He even bade farewell to the babe and resolved to stay clean till he was sure there was no heat on him.

He even considered leaving Chicago and was giving this serious thought over a drink in his favorite bar, when the two heavies appeared beside him.

One of them was heavily muscled, a snake's head tattooed on his right bicep, the other was bald, clean shaven, and shaped like a human battering ram.

Maximus's hands trembled; he knew what their presence meant. Aristo had connected the dots.

He forced a smile. 'Fancy seeing you guys here. A drink?'

Snake's Head grabbed the drink from Maximus's hand, pushed it across to the bartender, and shoved the lifter ahead of them out of the front door.

Bald held open the door to a dark van, bundled Maximus inside, while Snake's Head eased his bulk into the driver's seat.

The van sped off, jostling Maximus in the back. The lifter examined his confined space. There was no way to escape. There were no rear windows; the van could be opened only from the outside.

He tapped the partition, a darkened window slid open to reveal Bald's glittering eyes.

'Can we talk about this? I can pay you better than Aristo. You guys never need to work again.' Maximus hated the whiny tone in his voice, but he was past caring.

His life was numbered in hours and if whining was what it took to extend it, so be it.

Bald said something to Snake's Head and chuckled. The window slid back leaving the lifter in darkness.

Maximus knew where they would take him – an abandoned warehouse in Fuller Park that doubled as Aristo's playground.

It was here that he toyed with his victims before killing

them. The warehouse had iron girders, rusty chains, a crane that still functioned, hooks, and pointed things that were a killer's delight.

Maximus yelled and shouted and pleaded at the dark window. It stayed shut.

The van took a violent right that threw Maximus against the door but before he could recover, something smashed into its rear, flinging him against the partition.Zeb leapt out of the smoking SUV even before its engine had died. The van was still rocking on its wheels and from its passenger side emerged a bald man, shaped like a battering ram.

The man looked left, looked right. He spotted Zeb. His right hand flickered to his jacket.

Zeb shot him in the right shoulder, the silenced report lost in the sounds of the small street.

The man charged as if the .45 bullet was a mere fly, as if the spreading red blob on his body was paint.

Zeb sidestepped, slipped in a puddle of water. Arms made of steel were around him before he could recover.

He was rammed against the van. He lost his Glock. The shaven head butted into his chest with the force of a pile driver. He saw black for a moment.

Zeb brought his knee up when he got his breath back. The attacker took the impact on his thigh.

Another man emerged from the van, dressed in black with tightly-packed muscles that rippled, biceps that strained against a tight T-shirt, a snake head tat on one arm.

The second lowered the gun he was holding when he saw Zeb was captured. He smiled.

The smile faded and a look of shock crossed his face a second later. He looked down blindly at the spear sticking through his chest.

Knife. Not a spear. A Benchmade that had been strapped to Zeb's thigh a few seconds before.

His left hand had drawn and thrown it in a move that practice and the heat of innumerable battles had perfected.

A move that one mistake by the first attacker had enabled. His steel grip had been too high on Zeb, giving his captive's arms the freedom to move.

The second hood clawed at the knife, lost his balance, fell, striking his head against the van as he went down.

Zeb's attacker turned his head a fraction to see what was holding his partner up. A second that left his ear exposed.

A second was all that Zeb needed. He bit the hood's ear off. The man screamed. His grip slackened.

Zeb's right elbow caught him on his temple. A knife edged hand crushed the hood's throat and he stumbled back. Zeb shoved him away, letting him fall in the puddle.

In two steps he was at the knifed man who was desperately tugging at the deeply buried Benchmade. He coughed in agony, his fingers scrabbled on wet concrete.

Zeb looked down at him pitilessly, thought for a moment about killing him.

Leave him be. Let Churchey know.Maximus fingered his nose gingerly. It was swollen from the impact against the partition but didn't seem to be bleeding.

He rapped the partition several times. 'Hey, what's up? If y'all are going to kill me, there are easier ways.'

The driver, Snake's Head, swung his head sideways for a moment but didn't reply.

Maximus watched him; the dude was listening to what was happening outside. Maximus took his cue and jammed an ear against the van's sidewall.

Nada. 'What's happening?'

He got a reaction this time, but not the one he wanted; Snake's Head swore loudly and jumped out of the van.

Maximus tried the sliding door, it stubbornly remained shut. He cocked his head and got the muted sound of traffic.

He yelled at the top of his voice. 'Hello? Anyone out there?'

He jumped when something crashed into the side and a sliding sound came. He shouted again, beat the sidewalls with his fists.

Whoever was out there wasn't responding.

He drew a breath and prepared to launch another attack on the unyielding van when the sliding door slid open.

He yelped in surprise. 'You?'

The brown-haired dude from Damascus lasered him with a stare for a moment before moving to the front, checking it out to make sure it was clear.

Maximus followed him with blank eyes for a moment before realization flooded. He was free!

He whooped and started to clamber out when a hand shoved

him back.

'Wait here.'

The dude removed something from his jacket pockets, bent over Bald who seemed to be unconscious and cuffed his hands.

Unconscious and bleeding, Maximus noted when he saw the large stain on the hood's chest.

The dude checked out the other hood, didn't bother to cuff him.

'Is he dead?' Maximus couldn't control the quaver in his voice.

Give me a break, he remonstrated himself. *I came this close to dying.*

The dude's laser stare returned.

'You get to start again every day. Which way will you choose?'

The eyes seemed to burn inside him for a long second and then just like that, the dude turned and walked away without a backward glance.

'Hey, wait. What do I do now?' Maximus shouted.

The dude didn't reply. He ducked under a steel railing, crossed the street, and vanished.

Maximus hopped out, looked left, looked right, looked down at the two hoods. He kicked Bald for good measure, peered round the van, and hustled his ass away.

Later, much later, when he had checked into another hotel, using an alias, after he had showered, scrubbed and changed into new threads, once his favorite beer had coursed through him, the dude's words came back.

Maximus looked at the brew in his hand, at the way it caught the bar's lights and turned gold.

He made a resolution.

Straight and narrow, from now on. Zeb kept watch outside Maximus's hotel the whole night, watched him check out in the morning, check into another hotel and when evening fell, he ended his surveillance.

He'll be fine.

Aristo, on the other hand, won't be.

Chapter 9

Ajdan watched as Masis and Shiraz, his two fellow assassins, paced the living room of his apartment in Chicago.

The three of them lived close by and when news of Churchey's *accident* had reached him through the underground grapevine they had cultivated, he had summoned his partners.

The three of them went a long way back, trusted one another implicitly and undertook any new job or any decisive action only after consulting one another.

Most assassins were solitary animals; the three of them worked as a team, bringing complementary skills to the table.

Ajdan was the best shooter of them all and was their leader.

'We don't know if Churchey spilled your name.' The bristles on Masis's chin made a rasping sound as he ran a hand over them. He was the most cautious of them all; he played the role of devil's advocate.

'We don't even know if it was this Damascus guy who damaged Churchey.'

The Damascus guy was still unidentified. Ajdan's man had run his plates through the system, but those plates didn't exist. Ajdan had reported back to Boiler and had written off the guy.

Till now.

'Agreed,' Shiraz acknowledged Masis's point, 'but in our business, we can't make assumptions.'

Ajdan looked each one of them in the eye, got a nod in return.

That comment had sealed Churchey's fate. 'Where's my drink?' Churchey snarled at the bunch of people around him. One of his flunkies rushed out to find out; hopefully it would calm him.

Aristo Churchey was in a foul mood.

His right arm would take a month to heal and the stitches on his face itched. The dentist, who had worked on his teeth, had seemed to take an unholy pleasure in inflicting further pain on the gang boss.

His gang had turned Chicago apart but hadn't found a trace of the dude. Not a single camera in Churchey's home had recorded the guy.

On top of that Maximus had disappeared, one of his men was dead, the other, Bald, was shot.

Bald had confirmed it was the dude who had freed Maximus. 'Took us apart as if we were made of paper.'

The rage in Churchey blossomed on seeing Bald's pale face and hearing his weak voice.

He took his rage out on those around him. One of the women had her jaw broken, a flunky had his face rammed into a mirror.

His men kept asking questions, scouring bars, questioning hotels and motels with a description of the dude.

They didn't get any hits. It was as if the dude appeared and disappeared at will.A full bladder roused Churchey at night. He stumbled out of bed awkwardly, the sling around his neck restricting his movement.

He yawned and took a step to his bathroom when a faint noise came from outside.

He listened. He didn't hear anything.

He withdrew a handgun from a bedside chest and opened the bedroom door cautiously. Ever since the dude, security around his bedroom had been beefed up.

Three hoods stood guard at all times, three of his best men.

Churchey relaxed when he saw the three shadows. 'Everything alright, Carl?'

Carl grunted. Churchey let out the breath he had been holding, shut the door and went to the bathroom.

A relaxing five minutes later, he emerged, yawned, and lay down on his bed.

'What...?' He shouted and scrambled out of the bed on seeing the figure over him.

'Hello, Aristo,' Ajdan's smile had no humor in it. He pushed the gang boss back on the bed with a lazy hand.

'You've been telling tales.'

Churchey began screaming ten minutes later.Ajdan washed his hands in Churchey's bathroom an hour later.

Blood swirled in the sink for a few seconds and then was sucked away by the swirl of water. He patted his hair in place, emerged from the bathroom, glanced once at the dead gang boss and exited the bedroom through a window.

Masis and Shiraz were outside, waiting in a getaway vehicle.

The three of them had entered Churchey's mansion and had

taken out eight men on Churchey's floor.

They had planted alarms at the entrance to the floor to warn them of the arrival of Churchey's crew, and then Masis and Shiraz had left Ajdan alone with the gang boss.

Ajdan clambered down a drainpipe, signaled with a flashlight in the direction of the getaway vehicle, and when he got an answer, ran swiftly to the outer walls of the mansion.

The mansion had dogs. They had been drugged.

It had surveillance cameras. They had been hacked.

It had a roving patrol of three men. Ajdan had timed his entry and exit to coincide with their absence.

Penetrating Churchey's mansion hadn't been difficult.

Ajdan and his men had once breached the palace of an African dictator and had killed him in his sleep. That had been far more challenging.

He reached the wall, hauled himself up swiftly, ran on the balls of his feet to the open door.

He didn't exchange high-fives with his men. He didn't slap their backs. They were professionals.

Their anonymous sedan pulled away and it was only when three miles separated them from the mansion that the first word was spoken.

'Did he spill?' Masis asked from behind the wheel.

'Yes. But he didn't know anything. He described the man, but we already have him on the photographs.'

If his men were disappointed, they didn't show it. Professionals.

'Churchey?' Shiraz asked.

'Won't trouble us.'

Ajdan settled back and let Masis thread their way through winding streets.Zeb followed them, four car lengths behind, on a bike, a Yamaha, a common make in the city.

He knew Ajdan would make a move on Churchey; it was the way a professional worked.

His patience had been rewarded when the Ford showed up at two in the morning, circled the mansion once, parked in deep shadow, and three figures emerged.

Zeb stifled his disappointment when he saw the three figures were masked.

He watched them climb over the wall and after waiting for a few minutes, darted to the car and planted a GPS tracker beneath it.

He had already snapped a photograph of its plates and when he got back, he mailed Werner with the number.

Two men returned after forty-five minutes and another ninety minutes later, the third man returned.

The third man bent to enter the vehicle, ripped off his mask with a hand and for one second, his face was exposed to Zeb.

Pale complexion, dark, short hair, dark eyes, clean shaven. Zeb's phone captured it all and when the Ford swung out, he fell in behind.Traffic was light that time of the night, and even thinner on the streets that the Ford wended its way through.

Smart. They want to see if they've been made.

Zeb had killed his lights on the black Yamaha, but he dropped back further, as they moved from neighborhood to neighborhood.

West Town fell behind, Near West Side drifted past. They meandered through New City in no particular hurry, a Ford leading the way, two other sedans in between, the dull black Yamaha bringing the rear.

The Ford's flasher lit and it hung a left into a narrow street. One car followed it, and so did Zeb, coming up from far behind.

He had a street map of the city on a console on the bike; the GPS tracker lit up on it in green flashes.

The street opened into a four-way junction; he crouched lower, prepared for a sudden maneuver.

The move, when it came, caught even him by surprise.

A hand came out of the Ford, something liquid splashed on asphalt. The car in between swerved suddenly, lost control, mounted the pavement and crashed against a lamp post.

Oil or something else.

Zeb took evasive action, but it was too late. His bike lost purchase, skidded and just before it crashed into the middle car, he flung himself away.

He rolled and came to rest behind a short flight of concrete steps that led to the entrance of a dark apartment block.

He rose, ducked back swiftly, when a gun chattered, another one followed. *HK and an Uzi.*

The rounds tore into concrete, bit off small chunks, flung them against empty space and unmoving walls.

The bursts came to a stop, an engine growled and silence fell over the street.

Not for long, however, as lights came on in the apartment block, windows raised and heads poked out.

Zeb peered out, saw that the Ford had disappeared. He ran to his bike, saw it was not badly damaged, reversed directions and went back the way he had come.

The GPS tracker still shone on his console and beckoned at him. It was moving faster now, just on the edge of West Englewood. He paused for a few moments, withdrew a can of white paint from his backpack, sprayed it on the Yamaha's tank and resumed the chase.

The paint proclaimed itself to be a quick drying one. Even if it didn't, there was enough of it to give the bike a white on black appearance, at a quick glance.

He caught sight of them in Chatham, fell behind them, followed them for three miles more before he gave up the chase.

The Ford now contained three black youths who frequently thrust their heads out of the windows and shouted whatever men under the influence of alcohol shouted.

Ajdan and his men had given him the slip.Dirk and Jane's bodies were discovered a week later.

A search party for them had gone out the next day after their disappearance, but hadn't found any traces of them.

They hadn't visited their usual haunts in Frederick, nor had they holed up with any friends. Intermittent rain made the search difficult and had washed away any tracks there were.

It was only when a bunch of hikers stumbled across the grave that the bodies were discovered.

The killing flagged Sarah Burke's attention and she and Mark Kowalski were in Buckeystown the next day. She took one look at the bodies, made a few calls and the investigation got transferred to the Feds.

She and Kowalski interviewed all employees at the catering business.

All they got was a description of a man who had met Dirt Beatty. Average height, light hair, grey eyes, no visible tattoos, clean shaven.

'Around ten million men will go by that description,' Kowalski cursed under his breath.

No one had overheard the conversation; no one had spotted any strange vehicle.

The lady at the gas station said a stranger to the parts had filled a new SUV; he was tall, bald, green eyes, hollowed cheeks.

Oh and he didn't speak. She tried to engage him in conversation, it was the neighborly thing to do in Buckeystown. But did he respond? No.

She shook her head. It was a sign that the country was coming to no good end when people stopped being polite to one another.

'Ma'am, do you have the SUV's plates?' Burke interrupted her.

The white-haired lady's eyes grew wide. Why would she note that? The man had paid good money. So what if he didn't have manners.

Burke gave up and went outside the gas station, Kowalski following her. Her mood darkened when she noted there weren't any cameras at the store.

She went back to the catering store, asked the bunch of gathered people there if any of them had spotted a new SUV. A couple of residents scratched their chins thoughtfully.

Yeah, they had, now that they thought of it. New vehicles were rare in the town, especially new SUVs.

Nope, they hadn't noted the number. 'It could be a serial killer,' Kowalski said morosely as he dug into his salad and chewed it savagely.

They were back in Washington D.C. after a frustrating week spent in Buckeystown and Frederick.

A week in which the killers' trail just died, as if they had vanished in thin air.

On top of that, the unspoken but obvious resentment from the local agencies – the state police, the sheriff's office – at having their case yanked away, added to the pressure Burke and Kowalski were facing.

Seeing no possibility of further progress, they had retreated to D.C. to figure out their next steps.

They had run the victims through all their databases. Their lives didn't intersect. All of them had led clean lives, not even a speeding ticket among all of them.

A day's brainstorming with their team got them no further and when Kowalski had suggested a feeding break, they had all jumped to it.

'It's not.'

Kowalski started, spilled sauce on his shirt, cursed under this breath and looked up to see Carter sliding smoothly, silently, into a chair next to him.

'How did you find us here?'

Carter ignored him, looked at Burke. 'You know it's not a serial killer.'

'I know nothing of that sort.' She tried to keep the waspishness out of her voice.

Carter's habit of appearing out of nowhere unnerved her. She had tried to find out who he was but other than a bland profile of his and his security consulting firm, she hadn't got much.

She asked Pierce who shrugged. 'All I know is Pat vouches for him. You can ask Pat.'

She had asked the director and hadn't got far. She began again. 'We are investigating all avenues–'

The look on Carter's face silenced her. 'You know what's common about these killings?'

Kowalski snorted. 'Other than no motive, you mean?'

Burke gave him a look to silence him, turned back to Carter. 'No apparent motives. Small town killings. Tortured. Cut brutally. Victims are all young, in their mid to late thirties.'

Carter kept looking at her when she had finished.

'What?'

Carter didn't reply. She ran through the details in her mind. Nope. She had got all the similarities.

'You got something else, Mr. Carter?' Kowalski asked with elaborate politeness.

Carter's hand disappeared inside his jacket. He placed three photographs on the table. The victims from the three towns.

Burke glanced at them. Raised her eyes at Carter. 'We've seen them.'

Carter didn't reply. He pushed them toward her with a finger.

She frowned, looked again at the pictures. *What have I missed? What's he seeing?*

She detached her mind, closed down the ambient sounds in the restaurant, let her vision blur a little and looked again.

Seconds felt like minutes, but she got no closer. Her hair flew around her face when she shook her face in irritation and looked up at Carter.

He re-arranged the photographs. The men at one side, the women at another.

She glanced down, sucked in her breath sharply. Kowalski's muttered something, a curse. He had gotten it too.

'They look the same at first glance.' She turned to Kowalski. 'How did we miss that?'

There was no recrimination in her voice. Burke was successful not just because she was good. She was also an excellent manager of people; she didn't play the blame game.

'The killer is hunting someone, someone who looks an awful lot like the dead. Someone who lives in small towns.'

Burke stared off in the distance, letting her thoughts fall into place. 'Parker and the New Jersey killings weren't who he was seeking.'

She turned sharply at Carter; saw the grim look on his face.

If the Beattys weren't who the killer was after, there would be other victims.

Unless they found him.

Which, going by what they had, wasn't a very high probability.

'Did you get anything from the Damascus site?' Carter broke her train of thought.

'A rough description of the man in Beatty's store and that of another stranger in the town.'

She turned her tablet computer around, swiped on the screen and brought up a couple of sketches.

Gone were the days of an artist drawing by hand. Now police forces and investigative agencies used technology to draw up likenesses.

Carter stared at the two pictures for a moment, handed back her tablet.

'A few million men would fit that description, wouldn't they?' Burke smiled ruefully. 'That's the story of this investigation.'

Silence fell over them which was eventually broken by Kowalski.

'What's your interest in this, Mr. Carter?'

Carter didn't answer for a moment. The faraway look in his eyes disappeared only when he sensed the questioning looks from the FBI agents.

'Hank Parker was a friend.'

'We went through his contacts, his phone numbers, his

computers. There wasn't a Zeb Carter listed on any of those. Were you in the Army with him?'

'Yeah.'

'Strange. We checked his Army records too and contacted all those he had served with. Your name didn't come up.'

'Who exactly are you, Mr. Carter?' Burke tried but couldn't hold back the sharp tone.

She was used to doors opening, witnesses opening the tap of information, as soon as she uttered the magic three letters *FBI*.

Carter? He just didn't seem to care. After Carter had inserted himself into the Damascus investigation, she had come across Director Murphy after a meeting and had questioned him about the man opposite her.

The FBI Director had been evasive.

'Carter is a good friend to us.' He had left it at that.

She had requested Carter's Army records and after reading the one that came through, had made further enquiries. Instead of receiving more information, she had received a one line email from Murphy.

'You won't find anything more on him.''Did you and Parker work in some secret unit?' She smiled to lighten the question.

Carter gave her his now-familiar impassive look and prepared to rise.

'Surely you can tell us, Mr. Carter. It could help the investigation. We are on the same side after all.'

Carter didn't reply.

She paused a beat, tried again. 'We are, aren't we?'

Something turned in the dark eyes. 'Not really. You hunt folks down, put them behind bars.'

'I hunt folks down, put them beneath the ground.'

Chapter 10

Someone else is doing the killing?
Zeb leaned back in the Gulfstream, as it accelerated down the short strip of concrete and parted ways with the earth. The capital city circled lazily in his window, became smaller and disappeared when the aircraft pointed its nose at Chicago.

The luxury airplane was a gift from a Saudi royal who he had helped in a previous mission; the two pilots in the cockpit were ex-servicemen he had served with and trusted.

He brought up the images from Burke's computer in his mind. *Nope, haven't seen them before, either.*

Could they be the assassins' men? Assassins are generally loners or work as a small team. But these guys could be different.

The plane banked, sunlight entered and with it came another thought.

Could they be Churchey's men?

Churchey is dead.

But maybe his gang is still hunting me.

Only one way to find out.

Churchey's men found him.

At O'Hare, Zeb flagged a cab, tossed his backpack in the rear, gave his hotel's address to the driver and settled back.

He was lost in thought, trying to fit the pieces together, and missed the driver adjusting his mirror. He missed the driver's half turned head. He ignored the mumbled conversation in the front.

It was only when the cab crawled to a halt at a light that he sensed it.

Something about the way the driver sat.

His eyes lingering too long on his, in the mirror. The elaborate trying-to-be-casual gestures.

He looked at the driver's picture on the board stuck to the partition. No memories surfaced.

It came to him when the driver glanced at him again.

Churchey's gang! They must have a network of cab drivers who act as look-outs.

He extended his arm casually, withdrew his Glock from his backpack and tucked it under his thigh.

The cab hung a right and when the driver was distracted, he swiftly donned his shoulder holster.

How will it go down?

Driver will call in. Gang will send men.

Where?

Has to be somewhere in public. Some place the gang owns.

They got stuck in rush hour traffic, behind office workers and school buses, delivery vans, and sandwich trucks.

The driver looked furtively in the mirror, made another call, and when the line of gleaming metal started moving, he turned on his left clicker, and moved to the outer lanes.

'Gotta fill up,' he called out over his shoulder.

'Sure. Take your time.'

A gas station. Makes sense. Perfectly innocuous. The gang probably owns several all over town. Good front for money laundering.

The driver ignored the first gas station, which bore a prominent oil maker's brand and eased into the next one. It had faded signage, its pumps were grimy, but the windows were clear and clean.

The driver stepped out, went to the rear of the cab, uncapped the tank and began fueling.

Zeb looked around the station; six pumps, of which five were occupied. The cab took the remaining spot, right at the front.

Smart. No other vehicles will enter. The other cars are behind me.

He looked inside the store, thought he saw bodies moving inside, but couldn't be sure.

He removed a pair of shades from an inside pocket, flicked a switch on one of the stems and a screen opened on the inside of his sunglasses.

The Ray-Bans were fitted with pinhole cameras that looked backward, in the rear of the stems. A switch turned them on and off; when on, the cameras displayed the rear view in high definition.

The driver came out, behind him came two other men. The three of them laughed, one of them high-fived the driver.

The three spread out, two of them going to cars behind Zeb, the driver approaching the cab.

The station's door opened, a head poked out, a voice shouted.

The driver turned, replied, glanced back at Zeb apologetically and headed back inside.

The two men will circle and come from behind.

The screens on his shades were motionless for a moment, then two men appeared on them. They nodded at one another, spread out, walked to the cab.

The one on my right will make the first move, when he does, the one on the left will cover him.

The driver will then emerge, purely as back up. Two men will be enough.

Most times.

The man on his right quickened his pace, disappeared behind the rear pillar of the cab.

Zeb pictured it in his mind.

Left hand reaching for a gun inside his jacket.

Right hand reaching for the door.

Head bending.

One last glance at the other hood to check that he was in position.

Fingers spread out to grip the handle.

Zeb lashed out with his feet, slid out of the cab like lightning.

The door flung open as if rocket propelled, caught the hood on his chin and knees.

He groaned, crumpled, and fell.

His gun clattered, bounced once.

Zeb kicked it away, followed it up with a kick to the gangbanger's groin.

Out of action.

Movement.

The other hood stopped his forward motion, changed direction to come behind Zeb.

The beast flared from somnolence to action in a nanosecond, filled Zeb, powered his left arm, vaulted him over the roof of the cab, his body low, gliding through a thin layer of air.

His right arm came up, the Glock at the end of it.

His vision narrowed. The cab disappeared. The gas station blurred.

Only the hood remained.

The look on his face changed from startled to desperation to panic. His gun arm turned to take in Zeb.

A flower blossomed on his right shoulder, darkened.

Another flower, this time on his left.

He fell back, the gun clattering on the ground.

Zeb landed, kicked the gun away, crushed the hood's wrists, and took cover behind the cab.

His Glock moved in straight lines, narrow arcs, no wasted movement.

It covered the gas station's door, through which the cab driver burst wildly, his mouth wide, shouting incoherently.

The shotgun in his hands turned. Its barrel swung slowly, seeking for Zeb.

The Glock lowered an inch. Found his shoulder.

Bottom of breathing cycle.

A depress -.

'POLICE. DROP YOUR GUNS.'

Zeb's finger relaxed.

'DROP YOUR GUNS. NOW!'

His shoulders relaxed, his eyes didn't stop watching the driver.

The driver's eyes moved behind Zeb.

'DROP THEM NOW.'

His shotgun fell.

Zeb dropped his Glock, stepped a foot away from the cab, his eyes still watchful, still on the doors to the gas station.

The first cop came in his sight, then another, the two of them flanking him, their guns trained on him.

'RAISE YOUR HANDS. STEP BACK.'

Zeb raised his hands, stepped back only when the cab driver was surrounded and a bunch of cops had rushed inside the gas station.

Ajdan was in the kitchen, cooking a simple meal for the three of them. Rice, boiled eggs, lentils, three bottles of Newcastle Brown Ale.

A shout came from the living room.

He raised his head.

The shout came again. He wiped his hands on a towel and went outside.

Masis pointed silently at the TV and raised its volume.

The presenter's voice was breathless with excitement. 'Reports are coming in of Chicago P.D. stopping a gunfight at a gas station just a few minutes back. Two men are said to have been injured. Our reporter, Harry Deitch, is onsite and has more for us. What can you tell us, Harry?'

The camera panned to take in the gas station which was now filled with cruisers and TV vans. Ajdan's eyes narrowed when he saw the signage on the gas station.

'That's Churchey's isn't it?'

Shiraz bobbed his head in acknowledgement.

Ajdan punched numbers on a secure phone, his eyes never leaving the TV.

'Those are your men?' He asked when a voice came on.

A gangbanger, who was known to the cops as Louie Rivera, had been third in command when Churchey had been around.

He had taken over the gang by killing two rivals to the leadership. It didn't make any difference to the hoods on the street. They still ran women, pushed narcotics, and collected the money.

Ajdan held the phone away when the voice rose and ranted for a minute.

'Where are they now?'

He ended the call when Louie answered, tossed the phone on a couch.

'It's him.'

They watched the TV for several moments and just as Masis was turning it off, the scene shifted to the Chicago P.D. headquarters.

Another reporter appeared on the screen, gave more updates, recited the names of those arrested.

Masis's fingers stilled on the remote when the last name came up.

Zeb Carter.

Zeb was released six hours later. He was questioned several times by several cops, had stuck to his story of a security consultant visiting the city, who had been held up by the thugs.

The cops tried to break him down, tried to make him veer from his story. He didn't.

They said the hoods had spilled everything; that he had been harassing their gang, that he was responsible for Churchey's death.

Zeb gave them the look. They would believe the words of gangbangers over that of a reputable security consultant?

He gave them references. One of those names gave the cops pause.

It was that of the NYPD's Commissioner. Zeb knew that

the Chicago P.D.'s Superintendent was good friends with the Commissioner.

The cops disappeared and when they appeared hours later, he was free to go. All charges against him were dropped.

Zeb stared at them incredulously. 'All charges dropped?'

'Which part of that didn't you get?' A tired cop answered.

Zeb left before they changed their mind.

He stepped outside and was surrounded by cameras, reporters clamoring for a sound bite to fill the evening news.

He thought for a second, addressed the closest reporter. 'I am Zeb Carter.'

Masis watched him from a distance.

Ajdan had assigned him to follow Carter, the moment his name was revealed on screen. Now the name uttered by Herb Parker matched the face that had followed them.

The next step was to follow him, grab him, and question him.

Unbeknownst to them, it was the same question Sarah Burke had posed at Zeb.

Ajdan and Shiraz were on a call with their hacker the moment Masis left.

The hacker now had a name, with details, to go after.

Masis waited patiently, the bill of a ball cap covering his face, his jacket turned up, as the man named Zeb Carter recited his story to the press.

He answered questions, laughed readily, smiled disarmingly.

Masis held his phone up, zoomed the camera in and saw that the smile never reached Carter's eyes.

They were cool, seeking, looking beyond the banks of the cameras.

Searching for him!

Chapter 11

Zeb was taking his time with the bank of reporters thronging around him. Normal behavior was to avoid the press, avoid interviews, escape the glare of cameras, and keep a low profile.

During the six-hour incarceration he had come to a decision. The assassins would want to know what he knew. He would give them all the opportunity to find out.

The late Churchey's men wanted petty revenge. He wouldn't disappoint them; after all he wanted to know if vengeance was their only motive.

He would be bait.

He spent an hour answering all questions, working the media, ensuring that his name would be flashed in the hourly news.

Seven hours since I was arrested. Enough time for my hunters to deploy men.

His inner radar was quiet. He expected it to be. The assassins were good. The gangbangers wouldn't come anywhere near the police headquarters.

He meandered aimlessly once the news pack had moved off, stopping to eat at a food truck, using the polished steel front of the truck to watch his back.

No one ducked out of sight suddenly. No passersby turned around.

He walked aimlessly down East Thirty Fifth Street, past the usual crowd that hung around a police station. Families, ambulance chasers, hoods, the curious, and the indifferent.

He stood for a moment opposite a college, a research institute, watched as earnest-looking men and women disappeared into its campus, kids who wanted to, and someday would, change the world.

He turned corners, headed down South State Street, was tempted for a moment to catch the bus that came fuming and snorting, all gleaming metal and chrome.

No bus. Will be crowded.

He paused when he stepped on the lush green of Stateway Park, closed his eyes to the sun and felt it warm deep inside him.

The beast slumbered. His radar was quiet.

The guys I saw were good. Very good. They would know how to stalk without signaling it.

A Frisbee landed at his feet. A pigtailed girl came chasing it. He tossed it back to her and got a gap-toothed smile in return.

A shout turned his head.

A football match. Bare-chested men wrestling and grunting as they wrestled on lawn for possession of an oval ball. The battle instinct watered down and shaped with rules as humans moved out of caves, stopped using cudgels, farmed and built towns, then great cities.

He walked deeper, once again wearing his Ray-Bans, turned on the switch and the screens lit up as if by magic.

A family behind him. A lone man. Zeb watched him for some time. The man sat down, removed a sandwich box from a backpack and a bottle of beer.

Not him.

A man hailed him as he walked deeper inside. A black man, seated, at a small table.

Zeb approached him, curious, and when he got closer he saw the man had a white beard that caught the sun and shone silver.

The thick curly hair on his head was grey, his shirt and shorts had seen better days, the loafers on his feet were scruffy.

It was his smile that held Zeb's attention. It was wide and genuine and tugged at something inside him. The black man's eyes twinkled and his hand waved at the seat opposite him.

It was then that the small table caught his attention. Neatly laid out on it was a small carpet of black and white squares on which were miniature pieces.

A chess board. A game that originated in India that took battle away from the heat and dust of the plains and brought it into the living room. A battle without loss of life.

Zeb was surrounded by chess players.

Bwana and Bear were aces at the game, but the twins and Roger weren't far behind. The best of them all was Clare. Her hobby was playing online against grandmasters from different countries.

Zeb got his ass whipped every time he played against them even though he wasn't a novice.

He glanced in his screens again.

No one approaching threateningly. I'll give them time.

Zeb took the offered seat, placed a ten-dollar bill next to the board, saw the appreciation in his eyes,

The man reached a hand out. 'Casper, sir. Chess king of this park. How may I beat you today? Slow or fast?'

Zeb shook the proffered hand. 'Zeb. Defeat doesn't care about speed does it?'

Their first moves were cautious, each testing the other out, taking time to think several steps ahead.

Zeb checked his screens periodically. They didn't indicate danger.

Have I been wrong?

He sacrificed a pawn, at which Casper grinned. 'You aren't going to draw me in like that, sir.'

'Zeb.'

Casper shook his head. 'This is battle, sir. We treat our opposition with respect, with formality.' His black eyes twinkled. 'It'll be Zeb when you beat me and we share a drink.'

Zeb paused, looked at him with narrow eyes.

How did I miss it?

Casper had the look.

'Where?'

Casper sat back and returned a thoughtful gaze. ''Stan. Two tours.'

Zeb moved. He counter-punched. Zeb trapped his knight, he escaped.

'You?'

Zeb shrugged. 'All over.'

Casper considered him for a long moment, nodded finally.

Two men appeared at the bottom of the screen. Zeb glanced at them. One of them was pushing a baby carriage, the other was talking animatedly at him.

Not them.

'Why this?' He asked Casper.

'I came back to a different country, sir. My wife had run away with someone else, taking our child along with her. I was denied visitation rights. I was left with no family. I didn't have a home. There weren't any jobs. I was good at chess; it was better than lying down on the street with a placard in hand.'

There was no bitterness in his voice, just calm acceptance, a steely resolution in the tone.

Zeb looked down to find a knight captured.

He attacked. Casper fell back.

The two men with the baby were now in the center of his screen. A hundred yards behind his left shoulder. There were lone figures in the distance, none of whom came closer.

He captured his first victim, Casper's knight, in a complex move Bwana had taught him. Casper sucked in his breath, rocked back and studied the board.

'You've done this before.'

Zeb didn't reply.

The baby chair came at the edge of his vision, then the two men.

The beast was silent.

He glanced casually at them, watched them draw parallel.

The animated man turned as if he felt the weight of Zeb's gaze, locked eyes with him for a second.

He moved on, Zeb turned back to the board.

He played distractedly, paid the price when Casper toppled a bishop.

'You got to be focused, sir.'

Casper's voice came at him from a distance.

He looked up.

The animated man was looking back at him.

Zeb moved without conscious thought, rising, toppling his stool, taking a step sideways.

The animated man broke away and fled when Zeb burst into a sprint.

'What's up?' Casper yelled.

'It's called a retreat,' Zeb shouted and increased his pace.

The man, as tall as Zeb, dark-haired, ducked and weaved around the stragglers in the park, moving easily, as If floating just above the ground.

Zeb narrowed the gap, gauged the distance, dived at the man's legs.

The man turned, but not fast enough, fell, lashed out with one arm and a leg.

Zeb parried, attempted a wrist lock.

The man evaded it with ease. His other hand came up, something glinted.

Zeb knocked the handgun away before it had lined up. It skittered through the grass, came to a rest a few feet away.

The man lunged, rained blows, one of which caught Zeb on the side of his head.

Then he was up, away, running.

Zeb followed.

The gap had increased. *I can still bring him down before he leaves the park.*

The man swerved, headed to the pigtailed girl, grabbed her and shoved her blindly in Zeb's direction.

Her thin scream sounded. She stumbled. Started falling.

Zeb skidded on grass, reached her before she hit the deck. He righted her. Turned her in the direction of her folks.

Turned back to the fleeing man.

He had slowed to look back.

Zeb moved.

The man ran.

This time he headed to a couple.

They scattered, but he went closer to them.

'Keep away,' Zeb shouted, but it was too late.

The man's arm flashed once, and then he ran away, a burst of speed putting distance between him and the couple.

The woman fell. Her panicked screams filled the air.

Zeb reached her, bent over her.

Her right side was turning red.

He ripped the lower part of her shirt, fashioned it into a compress and applied it to her.

'Call 911,' he commanded her partner who was hovering above him, joined by several onlookers.

A man thrust forward through the growing crowd, announced that he was a physician. Zeb left the woman's care to him and made his way back and out of the crowd.

The attacker was long gone.

He searched in the grass for the fallen gun and when he found it, picked it up by a thumb and forefinger, hunted around till he found a discarded plastic bag, wrapped it around the gun and pocketed the evidence.

Any prints on it will be useless. He's a pro. He knew I would go to the assistance of the girl and the woman.

But maybe all was not lost. He extracted his phone.

Masis paused behind a food truck across the street from the park and peered back.

He could see no sign of Carter. A crowd had collected around the wounded woman; presumably it had swallowed Carter.

He discreetly wiped perspiration away from his forehead and made his way swiftly down the street, sticking to crowds, blending in.

Just another harried office worker hurrying from point A to

point B.

He turned a corner and headed deep into a less crowded alley. Behind a large trash can, he withdrew the knife, inserted its blade in a crack in the pavement and broke it. He made smaller pieces of the knife and pocketed them.

They would be disposed of later.

He had lost his gun. It didn't matter.

Ajdan, Shiraz and he had burned their fingertips several years back and had surgery performed.

They no longer had identifiable fingerprints. They had smudges which were unintelligible to fingerprint recognition devices. They had killed the surgeon.

Fool. He cursed himself and used stronger words in Armenian.

Carter hadn't made him but when he had looked back the second time and had seen the dark, probing eyes, something in him had given. Years of discipline broke and he had fled.

Of course Carter would follow.

It was only his swift knifing that had held up Carter.

He pulled out his phone and sent a short message to Ajdan and Shiraz.

Got held up. Can't make it to meeting.

The three of them had a code they used to communicate with one another. *Held up* meant that his assignment hadn't gone down smoothly. The second line told his partners to immediately abandon their apartments and go to another secure hide-out.

They had several such hideouts in the city.

He hadn't used a few keywords, which meant he was not under duress. Nor was he injured.

He wended his way to a department store, picked out a couple of items of clothing, ripped off the tags and went to a changing room. At all times, he kept his head bowed, away from prying cameras.

Masis looked different when he emerged. The muted orange jacket drew attention to him. But now his gait had changed, he walked on his toes, he projected confidence.

They were small things, but the human brain put them all together when identifying a person.

Masis wasn't the knife-man anymore.

He hung inside the glass doors of the department store and watched the outside world go by.

Carter didn't show.

He emerged, hailed a cab, gave an address.

He changed his mind when he was nearing it, gave another address.

He boarded a bus when he exited the taxi, and sat in it till it reached the end of its journey. He took another cab and returned to the department store.

He journeyed aimlessly for three more hours and when he was sure that Carter or any possible pursuer had been evaded or had died of boredom, he started for their hideout.

He walked the last three miles after alighting from the bus, joined the throng of people hurrying home.

A left turn, a straight-ahead, a mile after a right turn, brought him within two blocks of the apartment.

It was when he was crossing a darkened street that it happened.

A leg shot out.

He stumbled.

Chapter 12

He fell, rolled, immediately knowing who had tripped him up. He kept rolling, rose and faced the shadowed figure.

Carter!

He would recognize that posture anywhere.

He attacked, a flurry of blows aimed at Carter's throat, groin, and body. Carter sidestepped, parried some of them and counterattacked.

The city was silent, but for their harsh breathing. A solitary light threw their shadows on the wall, shapes that moved in a blur and sometimes merged in with the pavement.

His fist caught the side of Carter's neck, a satisfying grunt emerged, but before he could follow up, his hand was grasped and a lock was applied. He slipped and that helped break the lock.

He was off-balance for a moment; the hammer blow that caught him, threw him back.

Carter didn't follow through. 'I don't want to kill you.'

Masis's leg shot forward in a short brutal arc and brought down Carter. His leg swept back and forward, caught the falling man in the abdomen.

Carter seemed to bounce. He slithered back swiftly but before he could rise, Masis kicked his hands away and he fell prone.

Masis pounced on his back, removed the broken blade, its largest piece that he still carried and aimed it at Carter's neck.

It never reached its target.

Carter was rolling even as he was thrusting down; the sudden move threw Masis off.

Carter's hand swung. A block of concrete numbed Masis's left shoulder. Carter's hand!

The hand rose again.

Masis head-butted him.

Mistake!

Carter caught him around the neck with an arm lock.

Carter's arm flexed, choked the breath out of Masis.

'Who are you?'

Carter's voice was low, even, despite the exertion, and in that moment, with his breath being squeezed out slowly, Masis knew he would lose.

He jabbed ineffectively with the blade.

Carter parried it away.

Masis twisted his neck, trying to look his captor in the face.

There was no give.

We have a code. The words hammered inside him in tune with his rapid pulse.

Masis tried one last move.

He gathered his legs underneath him and heaved.

Carter was resolute, immobile.

We have a code. He pictured Ajdan and Shiraz, an apology swept through his mind.

His hand moved of its own volition and the blade buried itself deep inside his own neck.

Zeb released him immediately, tried to stem the flow of blood, but the assassin knew what he was doing.

The blade had cut through his carotid and was buried deep. It acted like a seal, dislodging it would pump the blood out in great spurts.

Zeb fumbled with his phone, started to dial 911 when the killer moved again.

He withdrew the short piece of steel, brought it down again, this time in his throat.

His glittering eyes looked back at Zeb in triumph, even as dark fountains spurted out of his neck and splashed on the wall and pavement.

Drops landed on Zeb's face. He ignored them.

'Who are you?' He asked urgently.

The killer's mouth opened soundlessly, his teeth shone briefly, but no sounds emerged.

Zeb stayed with him till the light faded from the killer's eyes.

He removed the GPS tracker from the back of the killer's neck, pocketed his phone, searched the rest of his body, found nothing else and emerged cautiously from the alley.

The GPS tracker was a wafer-thin, malleable shape that was enclosed in a skin-colored fabric that had adhesive on one side. It was designed to be slapped onto the human body stealthily, and once applied, was barely detectable.

Zeb had palmed the tracker the moment he had left Casper's chess table and during the grappling with the assassin, had managed to apply it to the back of his neck.

He had tracked the killer on his phone and had caught up with him when the signal approached the alley.

He wiped his face with the bottom of his shirt, and commenced a slow jog that would take him, circuitously, back to his hotel.

He went through a mental checklist as he ran.

Check out. Check into another hotel.

Burn clothing.

Trace prints on gun and blade.

Break down phone.

The killer's eyes stayed in his mind, as if mocking him. *You won't find anything on me.*

Three miles in his run, sweat streaming down his face, after having given it thought, Zeb agreed.

The man was a professional. But I have to try.

A day later, in another bland hotel, the TV spouted news of a man found dead in a deserted alley, with his throat and neck cut savagely.

The cops had no clues to go on and made the usual noises of progressing on all fronts.

They appealed to people come forward with information, and on that, Zeb turned off the TV and lay back on bed.

Werner had come back with several profiles of Armenian assassins. There was one problem with those profiles. Most of the assassins were either dead, or not in the U.S.

Is that all you can do? Zeb had typed at Werner.

I dig out information, I don't create it. The supercomputer replied.

He was sorely tempted to call Meghan or Beth. Or even Broker. They knew he was involved in something.

Werner kept track of all them via the GPS sensors in their clothing, and tracked news items related to any of his crew. It sent messages to his team whenever any of them featured in incidents.

His arrest was known to his crew and they had flooded his phone with text messages.

Rog and I can be on the next flight. Bwana had texted.

Nope. Zeb had replied.

Hotshot, it looks like you need us. Meghan had sent.

Nope.

It's clear you are helpless without us, Beth snarked.

He didn't answer.

Why did Chicago P.D. release you? A cell suits you. Broker chuckled.

Zeb ignored him.

He crossed his arms behind his head, watched the swirls in the ceiling. They made as much sense to him as whatever was going on.

He sighed and rose.

Time to visit D.C.

'That man is Zeb Carter.' Boiler knew that already. He watched TV, but he listened to his caller speak.

He had spoken to Ajdan earlier, had conveyed his sympathies at Masis's death. He knew Ajdan was hurting, but the pro that he was, he had updated Boiler on various events.

When he had hung up, Boiler knew all there was to know about Zeb Carter. Ex-Army, ran a security consulting business in New York. No links to Parker.

The way he had followed Ajdan and his men, and the way he had taken out Masis, showed he was no ordinary soldier.

Ajdan's hacker had probed, but hadn't come up with anything more.

'His last rank was Major, but that doesn't mean anything.' Boiler nodded, knowing what Ajdan was saying. If Carter was Special Forces, his Army record would be redacted.

It was likely Parker and he had served together, might have been good friends, though no such relationship had emerged from digging into Parker or Carter's backstories.

Boiler sat staring into space for a long while before he issued instructions to one of his men.

Carter wasn't really his problem. Not unless he interfered in the gang's affairs.

It was clear he was related in some way to Parker and was following up.

He had no connection to Cezar.

Ajdan could go after him if he wished. The assassin didn't believe in vengeance, he was a pro.

However, Masis had been a very close friend.

Not the gang's problem.

Boiler was interested in recovering their money. They had to go about it a different way. Killing people who looked like

Cezar hadn't gotten them very far.

'Send two or three men to visit those towns one by one. Find out more about those people.'

'Any update on Carter?' Burke popped her head over Kowalski's cubicle in their D.C. office.

'Nope.' The junior agent leaned back in his swivel chair with a sign of frustration. 'Chicago P.D. let him go despite our request to detain him. They didn't have much to hold him for, but still … now we have no idea where he is.'

The two FBI agents had planned to fly to Chicago the moment news flashed of Zeb's arrest. However, this time, they weren't able to secure one of the FBI's private jets and by the time they reached the airport a few hours later, Carter had been released.

'He knows more than what he's letting on.' Kowalski tossed a ball of paper into a bin and when he looked up, saw the tight look on Burke's face.

Carter had asked them to look into Parker's movements, to see if he had visited any East European country.

He had clammed up as usual and performed his disappearing act when they asked him why.

Nevertheless, they dug into Parker's travel; he had visited many countries, but not for several years and hadn't set foot in East Europe.

Burke's phone rang before she replied.

'Burke,' she snapped impatiently.

She stilled, her eyes widening. 'We'll be down, right away.'

She beckoned at Kowalski and walked away without seeing if he was following.

'Where's the fire?' He panted as trotted to catch up.

'Carter's here. Downstairs.'

An hour later, Burke ran her fingers through her hair for the umpteenth time, while Kowalski looked at Carter with a slack-jawed expression.

She pinched the bridge of her nose, closed her eyes, and regained a sense of control.

'Let me see if I got this right. You tangled with the most vicious gang leader in Chicago, witnessed three assassins kill him. You then faced off three gangbangers, got arrested for it, and it's only now you're telling us?'

'I didn't see them kill Churchey.' Carter's voice was mild.

Burke slapped a palm on the metal desk. Kowalski started at the report, but Carter didn't even twitch.

'Don't split hairs, Mr. Carter.' She glared at him. 'You saw them go in, come out, and the next thing we know, Churchey's dead.'

'How do we know you didn't kill Churchey?' Kowalski asked truculently. He wasn't just a pretty boy flunky. Carter had better realize it.

'You don't. You'll have to trust me.'

Burke couldn't control the strangled laugh that escaped her. 'Trust you! Lord knows what else you're holding back.'

'Now that you mention it, one of those assassins is dead.'

This time Sarah Burke, ace FBI investigator, sat slack jawed.

Carter rose, went to a water cooler in the room, poured two glasses of water and handed it to them

Burke emptied hers in one gulp and was proud when her voice came out steadily. 'Care to tell us how?'

Carter told them.

No one moved in the long silence that followed. A door slammed somewhere outside, muted voices came through the thick door and with that, Burke finally broke the stillness.

'You killed him.' Her voice was flat, hard. She glanced at Kowalski, who acknowledged her look and searched on his tablet for reports of the dead man.

'He killed himself.'

'It's true,' Kowalski interrupted her and turned around his tablet computer for her to read the article.

She skimmed it swiftly, then eyed her partner, who dug his phone out and made a call.

Carter sat through it, utterly relaxed. If he was perturbed that they were checking with Chicago P.D., he didn't show it.

'The crime scene was clean. No ID. No weapons. No prints. Fibers, some of which matched the dead man's shirt.'

'The others will match mine.'

'Where is it?'

'It's ash now.'

Burke straightened, flicked a glance at Kowalski who rose and circled Carter.

'Mr. Carter, you're under arrest. You'll –'

'For what?'

'For killing that man. For –'

'Who said I killed him?'

'You had an altercation with him. You confessed to it.'

'Did I?'

She slapped her forehead mentally. *This room isn't wired. Neither Mark nor I recorded him. A rookie would have done better,* she berated herself.

Carter's hand moved for the first time. It approached his jacket.

'Don't move,' Kowalski shouted and rose.

Carter didn't stop. The hand went inside the jacket.

'STOP.' Burke's voice was high and thin.

She and Kowalski flanked Carter, her eyes wary, her breathing shallow.

Carter's hand slid out.

'Relax. It's just a phone. My gun's at the check-in desk.'

Burke stood motionless, her heart thumping wildly, one hand still on her hip, close to her gun.

'Who're you calling?' Her voice sounded unnaturally loud.

'You'll see.'

He hung up, looked at the two chairs, at them standing, but said nothing.

Kowalski flopped in his chair, said something beneath his breath, something that suspiciously sounded like a string of curses.

Burke's pulse returned to normal and with it came a biting anger. 'You came this close to getting shot in a Federal building.'

Carter shook his head. 'Nope. You wouldn't have.'

She leaned forward, her rage bubbling, 'Oh yeah? Why wouldn't we?'

Grammar, Sarah. An annoying little voice in her head droned.

She gritted her teeth, ignored it and waited for Carter to respond.

'I could read it in your eyes.'

His voice was soft; he was still sitting relaxed. Assured.

Before she could follow through, the door opened.

Director Murphy walked in, took in the situation swiftly. He nodded at Burke and Kowalski.

'Leave us.'

Hunting You

Chapter 13

Burke went back to her cubicle, riffled through reports on her desk, tapped a few keys on her keyboard, gave up and sat back.

She wondered what the Director was discussing with Carter. She tried to work out their relationship. She glanced at her phone and was tempted to ask Bob Pierce. She rejected the thought.

I bet he's telling the Director how incompetent we are. How we've gotten nowhere.

The rage returned again.

I am a good agent. No, I'm a great agent. I will deal with Carter. I will see this through. I will crack this case.

Kowalski tapped on her cubicle. 'The Director wants us.'

She followed him to the room, steeled herself invisibly, entered the room and stopped suddenly.

She was prepared for many scenarios.

She wasn't ready for the sight of Director Murphy chuckling at something Carter said. The Director waved them in, gestured at two chairs.

'Zeb tells me you have made a lot of progress in the case.'

Burke's eyes flew to Carter's, met an expressionless face. She turned back to the Director.

'Yes, sir.'

What progress?

'It looks like there are some Armenian assassins involved? And this gang in Chicago?'

'Yes, sir.' She retold the story Carter had narrated and when the Director nodded approvingly, her belly unclenched.

Kowalski glanced at her when she skirted around Carter's skirmish with the dead assassin.

'We'll run his prints and see where that leads us.' Her eyes flicked in Carter's direction. 'Mr. Carter has promised to share whatever he finds.'

The Director nodded absently. 'None of these developments were in your reports.'

'I haven't had time, sir.' She replied as honestly as she could. *Besides, I didn't know them until a few hours back.*

Kowalski couldn't contain his curiosity any longer. 'Sir, Mr. Carter is quite evasive about who he really is.'

The Director smiled thinly. 'I believe he's a security

consultant.'

Kowalski began to protest, saw the flinty look in the Director's eyes, and held back.

The Director discussed a few more details, glanced at his wrist, rose, hugged Carter warmly, beamed approvingly at his agents and left.

'So, we have helped you a lot?' Burke looked at Carter. 'The FBI is your private investigation agency?'

'Yes, Ma'am, and no, Ma'am. I *did* share what I knew. But in return, please let me know about those prints.' With that, he too left the room.

Count to ten, Sarah. Deep breaths.

Burke didn't know she had spoken aloud till her partner laughed. 'You've got to admit. If it hadn't been for Carter, we would still be twiddling our thumbs.'

Zeb flagged a cab, directed him to Reagan airport and when he had settled back, he closed his eyes for a second in anger. At himself.

I could've handled all of that better.

The cab went through Georgetown and by the time it crossed the Potomac, he had regained his equilibrium.

At the least they'll follow up on the gun and on East European assassins. Saves me talking to a cocky supercomputer.

Marty Solano was a watcher.

He hung about airports such as Ronald Reagan or the one at Dulles, noted the comings and goings of senators, various government officials, businessmen and sold that information on a daily basis to a select bunch of recipients.

That most of the recipients used his intel for illicit purposes didn't bother him.

Heck, he, Marty Solano, former bagman from New York, was hardly an advertisement for clean living.

The bagman business and his hometown had become too hot and hence he had moved to the less stressful climes of D.C. and to his current occupation.

In his job as bagman, he had come across several politicians who didn't want their whereabouts at given points in time to be made public.

Marty had seen the opportunity in that, had contacted a select set of clients and when they bit, he was in business.

All he needed was a buttonhole camera, a cell phone, and the money poured in.

Sometimes he was asked to look out for specific people.

Like this guy Zeb Carter. He didn't know why. He didn't care what for. He had a picture of Carter on his cell phone and he kept watch.

Marty was in a prime position – he would be. He knew the airport inside out and had snagged a spot facing the line of people who entered the security gates. He had found it was easier to hang around there, since people slowed down and gave him ample opportunity to spot them.

Carter was relatively easy to spot. For one, he was taller and leaner than most politicians. For the other, he had a particular bearing that Marty had seen in some soldiers.

Marty snapped his pictures, noted the time and sent them off to his clients.

His job was done.

The Gulfstream was with Broker who had to fly to Mexico on some Agency business.

That had constrained Zeb's movements, had made him fly commercial to D.C., and had led to Marty Solano spotting him.

He flew back to Chicago with one agenda in mind.

He had to talk to Louie Rivera, find out where the Armenians were holed up.

Ajdan got Carter's photographs from his contacts in New York. Those contacts worked like a brokerage business for assassins.

Assassins needed to know who was in which city on a given day. The brokerage business delivered, via their network across major airports.

He felt Shiraz's presence over his shoulder.

'He's coming back to Chicago. I checked the flight timings.'

'He's hunting us,' Ajdan turned to look at him.

'He doesn't know where we are. He'll go to Rivera.'

'Call him. Let's set up a welcome for Carter.' Ajdan's face was bleak, his eyes cold.

Masis had been with them for a long time. Shiraz and Ajdan had mourned silently, had ensured that his family would be taken care of.

They had decided to keep away from Carter, despite the loss of their friend, so long as their paths didn't cross.

However, Carter was now coming to their city.

Zeb went to the restroom on landing at O'Hare, disappeared into a cubicle, and when he emerged, Zeb Carter didn't exist.

The man who came out sported a brown moustache and had shoulder-length hair. He wore a loose striped shirt over blue jeans, scuffed sneakers and carried a yellow backpack.

He removed a cigarette from a case as he approached the airport's exit, held it between his fingers and hailed a cab.

'Where to?' the black driver asked him.

Zeb gave him the address of a downtown hotel where he was registered under a fake identity.

He checked in the hotel, emerged an hour later, hailed another cab and checked into a second hotel, an expensive one.

In the privacy of his room, he removed his disguise, turned the backpack inside out, back to its normal color and patched his laptop through the encrypted connection to Werner.

Rivera might be ready for me. Time to surprise him.

He asked Werner to provide him with a list of the gang's establishments. *No smart comments, please.* He crossed his fingers.

Werner responded minutes later. In plain, simple, language. He uncrossed his fingers.

Bars, nightclubs, warehouses, restaurants. Zeb went down the list, crossed out most of them mentally.

He brought up a maps program, placed the establishments on it and considered a few of them.

That warehouse looks promising.

It was in North Lawndale, on the corner of two streets and was ostensibly a furniture manufacturer's storage building. It had parking lots and unloading areas on the other two sides and no other buildings in its immediate vicinity.

It was high on Chicago P.D.'s radar for places to be watched and had been raided several times; but nothing incriminating had been found.

He went to a used car dealer, bought a Toyota Corolla that had seen better days and watched the warehouse for the next three nights.

He didn't see any signs of any gang. A couple of times he spotted unmarked police vehicles; however they didn't notice him.

On the fourth night, when the warehouse was empty, he

lobbed a smoke grenade through a window.

He stepped deeper into the shadows, pulled out his phone, called a number that Churchey had reluctantly given him.

He muffled his voice when his call was picked up. 'Your warehouse is going down.'

He ended the call, destroyed the sim card and the phone, produced his sat-phone and waited.

Forty-five minutes from his call, the first gangbanger arrived.

Three more cars arrived, packed with more hoods. They stood around gesticulating furiously before one man opened the warehouse and they streamed in.

That's my proof.

The next night, he lobbed five fire grenades and watched the warehouse burn.

Fire trucks raced in several minutes later and but despite their best efforts, the warehouse was destroyed. This time no gangbangers appeared.

The next day he went to a RadioShack, bought a drone, a burner phone and a sim card.

He assembled the drone in his room, tested it and when satisfied, lay down on his bed and slept.

His Corolla nudged out of the hotel's parking lot at two a.m. and meandered through the slumbering city.

When he was sure he wasn't followed, he drove to the late Churchey's mansion which was now occupied by Rivera, parked two streets behind it and proceeded on foot.

From behind an abandoned vehicle, he removed the drone, maneuvered it over and above the silent street, over the commanding walls of the mansion.

He upped the drone's speed once it was out of sight, headed back to his car and vanished in the night.

Rivera was roused by sudden shouting and a flurry of shots.

He rolled swiftly, grabbed his gun, and peered cautiously around.

He occupied Churchey's bedroom, had the same security set-up. The difference was he usually slept alone.

He *was* alone.

He knocked in a code on the steel reinforced door separating his bedroom from the hallway and got an acknowledgement.

He swung open the door, growled at hoods guarding his room. 'What's up?'

'Someone shot down a drone.'

He gave a disbelieving look at the hood, followed him downstairs, to the front yard where a knot of people had gathered.

They made way when he approached. He followed their gaze and peered cautiously at the device which lay mangled on the lawn.

'It's a drone,' he exclaimed, conveniently forgetting what his hood had told him.

A gangbanger came running up with another device, swept it across the drone, pronounced it free of bugs.

Another gangbanger approached it gingerly, lifted it up for all to see.

'There's a phone duct taped to it,' he exclaimed.

'It could be a bomb.' A voice murmured.

Most of the hoods shrank back.

Rivera glared at them, snatched the drone and removed the phone.

It was an old model; long before smart phones had conquered the world, phones such as these were in everyone's pockets.

He examined it. There were no numbers stored in it, the call log was empty.

His moved to toss it away when it rang.

Everyone froze.

He thumbed it on and held it to his ear.

'How many Ks did you have in the warehouse?'

Rivera held the phone away, glared at it as if it was human, and brought it back to his ear.

'Who are you?' His low voice had filled many a gangbanger with terror. It seemed to have no effect on the caller.

'I am Zeb Carter. I believe you are hunting for me.'

A murmur broke out from those close enough to hear.

Rivera waved them to silence. 'What do you want?'

'Where are the Armenians?'

'Armenians? I don't know any Armenians.'

A few hoods nodded approvingly.

He waited for a reply and when none came, he examined the phone. The call had been cut.

'Search the perimeter,' he ordered.

Hoods armed with AKs left and reported back half an hour

later.

'Clear.'

Rivera examined the drone again. It could have easily carried a bomb. This Carter had to be found and dealt with at the earliest opportunity.

'I want all motels and hotels searched in a ten-mile radius. Carter must be staying somewhere.'

He didn't wait to see if his command would be executed. It would be.

He turned away, seething in a quiet rage. He had lost a hundred Ks of meth, crack and various narcotics in the warehouse fire.

The drugs were concealed between the panels of the furniture in the warehouse. Whenever a shipment was to be made, the necessary pieces were unassembled, the drugs removed, and the furniture put back again.

He had bent cops in his payroll who warned him of any police raid. The warehouse was clean whenever the cops entered it.

The warehouse had earned the gang millions.

Its loss would cost him more than that. He had customers waiting for product, suppliers to pay.

He would rip Carter's balls off and stuff them down his throat.

Werner spat out a list of the gang's businesses; gas stations which had fake card readers, motels, bars and nightclubs, car washes, and loan sharking businesses. The list ran to two pages and these were just the known or suspected enterprises.

Zeb ran his eye down them, circled a few, looked them up on Google Maps and the next day, began his surveillance.

He rejected the gas stations after just an hour of watching. All of them had a few men hanging idly in the forecourts. Men who seemed to be just watching cars come and go.

Protection details.

The prostitution businesses were next. They were nothing but townhouses in the west side and south side of the city, where johns visited the women. The townhouses had been raided a few times, but it looked like the cops had given up.

Zeb sat in another car, this time a Sentra, watched the display on his laptop as a discreet camera shot the comings and goings continually.

He eventually rejected the townhouses too.

Too many people.

One of the loan sharking businesses was a possibility. It had a faded sign on the store that announced cheap loans. Through a glass front he could see a reception desk, cubicles, a couple of men inside.

Problem is, it's on a crowded street. Figures, the business needs foot traffic. Desperate people who are willing to take on extortionate terms and then realize, too late, that they have hocked their lives to the gang.

It was evening; people were hurrying home, smells drifted from food trucks and restaurants.

He parked the Sentra behind a pickup, joined the line behind a taco truck and sat on a bench as he kept watch.

He was prepared to give up on the loan business too. He dumped the paper wrapper in a garbage bin, stretched, then stilled when he saw the burly man exit the store.

His loose shirt swirled around his belly, the shape of a gun was briefly outlined.

He was flanked by two men who followed him closely.

Muscle.

Zeb's eyes lingered on the sack in the man's hand.

It came to him in a second.

The day's take from the store.

The three men headed to a SUV with darkened windows; one of the goons held the door open for the bagman, the other slid behind the wheel.

Zeb hustled to his Sentra, which was parked, luckily pointing in the same direction as the SUV.

The SUV merged into traffic with a blare of horns and squeal of tires. The Sentra fell behind it, two vehicles back.

The SUV went through Cicero, turned left on Oak Park, went through Mont Clare and Dunning and pulled up at a bar.

Bagman disappeared inside, empty handed, emerged carrying a notebook. The muscles remained in the SUV, guarding the sack.

Bagman went to five more establishments. Each time he emerged with just the notebook.

The day's take from each place, probably. Recorded in a notebook. No records on computers.

A plan began to form.

'He's hunting you,' Rivera strolled barechested in his mansion, a phone pressed to his ear, a flunky standing guard outside his room, Ajdan on the other end of the call.

He had left a message for the Armenian the day after the drone.

He had met the assassin along with Churchey, had inherited the relationship once Churchey had died.

Killed by Ajdan. He could kill me too. It was better to be cordial, maintain the business partnership.

Partnership. He liked those words. It gave him confidence. He now ruled the most fearsome gang in the city, but the Armenians were a different proposition.

Confidence mattered when dealing with them.

'No,' he replied in response to a query from Ajdan. 'We're still hunting him. He can't hide forever. This city is ours. Churchey was a fool. He should have gone after Carter with all the resources available to the gang.

Meaning: Rivera was not a fool. He would be more successful.

Ajdan hung up.

Rivera hung up.

'Where is he?' he asked his flunkies.

The bagman was sweating. It was end of the month. Wages usually ran out by now. Bills still had to be paid though. It was a good day for the loan sharks.

He paused for a second outside the store, took a deep breath, moved the sack from one hand to another, and went to the SUV.

Easily two hundred Ks in it. Mostly small bills, but that was good. The people they lent to did not have large bills.

The store didn't just lend. It collected too. People came every week, deposited what they owed, got a slip of paper as receipt, on which was also scrawled the amount they owed.

It was a proper business.

Those who didn't pay, were visited by big men. That was a proper business too.

The SUV drove away, forced its way through reluctant traffic, pulled outside the first bar.

Bagman disappeared inside, collected the notebook, and returned.

Second bar, the same procedure.

At the third bar, someone jostled into him from behind.

He cursed, turned back, saw a drunk weaving unsteadily.

He shoved the man back, swore at him.

He waved impatiently at one of the hoods that was exiting the SUV. To protect him.

Just a drunk. No harm.

The hood eased back in the vehicle.

The second hood opened the door for him, crowded behind him to hustle him inside.

Bagman had one leg inside, was heaving his body in, when a sickening clunk shook the SUV.

He turned.

He fell inside when the hood, now limp, cannoned into him.

A shape appeared and filled the door.

The drunk!

A gun appeared in the drunk's hand as if by magic.

The hood behind the wheel moved.

The gun moved. The hood backed down.

The gun waved again.

The hood reversed the vehicle.

The drunk spoke once, gave an address.

Bagman watched in sick fascination.

The wig disappeared. Something from his mouth came out, the cheeks collapsed.

Carter!

Bagman recognized him from the photographs Rivera had circulated.

He moaned in despair, didn't see the barrel move, and slipped into darkness.

The hood behind the wheel looked in the mirror.

Carter's eyes were on him.

His gun was in the seat beside him.

He could reach out, point it backward, pull.

'Whenever you're ready.'

Carter's voice was bored.

The hood decided to live.

It wasn't his money.

Chapter 14

Zeb directed the driver to the burned out warehouse, which was now deserted. Yellow tape still surrounded it, but onlookers had moved on, fire trucks had other fires to put out.

He felled the hood with his gun barrel, dragged him out, propped him against a wall.

He arranged the bagman next to the hood. The second hood was coming to, but sank into oblivion when Zeb kicked him.

He left the three of them against the ruins of the warehouse, bagman flanked by the two hoods. He went back to his Sentra, moved the money to the rear seat.

He looked down the street, found a convenience store, where he bought several paper bags.

He distributed the money into the smaller paper bags, brought up his map on which he had circled several establishments.

Three hours later several charities in Chicago received mysterious cash donations.

Rivera frothed and raged. He shouted and ranted and when he couldn't contain himself, he capped one of the hoods.

He turned his gun on the bagman who wet himself.

Rivera was about to pull when the phone rang. The one that Carter had sent.

'Did you cap them all?'

Rivera screamed. He flung the phone against a wall. It shattered, its battery slipped out and slid across the polished floor.

When calm had returned, an hour later, he got a hood to search through the pieces, find the sim card. It was inserted into another handset.

'Find him.'

He knew the words were meaningless. His men were searching flat out.

Carter was a ghost.

Zeb went to one of the gang's nightclubs, ordered a drink, and surveyed the establishment.

This time he was dressed as a businessman. Greying hair, flabby belly, scuffed shoes.

The security staff didn't give him a second glance. They went through his briefcase perfunctorily, found nothing but files and papers in it, and waved him inside.

Hoods. All over the place. Rivera will have beefed up security at all his businesses.

He found a bank of phones, discreetly wore a pair of flesh-colored gloves, placed a piece of hard candy in his mouth and dialed 911.

'There's a bomb in the Big Hippo,' he told the operator.

He left the nightclub, went to another SUV where he changed into a T-Shirt, jeans, and running shoes. He donned a ball cap and pulled its bill low, put on his jacket to hide his shoulder holster and waited.

The first cruiser screamed ten minutes later.

In half an hour the nightclub was evacuated.

He drove to the next establishment, a gentlemen's club, and closed it down.

By midnight, seven of Rivera's nightclubs had shut down. Some because of a bomb call, some because of suspected narcotics dealing.

Rivera was bleary eyed by the time the sky started to lighten. The seven nightclubs together took in close to a hundred Ks each night. Including the loan shark collection, he had lost over a quarter of a mil in one day.

One of the ever-present women handed him a steaming cup of brew. He snatched it, swallowed it and choked when the phone rang.

'Where are they holed up?'

'I'll kill you,' he screeched. 'I'll rip your –'

'You're not having much luck are you?' The cold voice cut through his ranting. 'I can keep on going and shut down all your businesses. It's up to you.'

Rivera stood breathing harshly, the brew forgotten in one hand. 'How do I know you'll not resume?'

'You don't.'

The bagman, sleeping on a couch, snored, while Rivera pondered.

Quarter of a million dollars.

'They were in Edison Park when I met them. This was a long time back.' He gave Carter the address of an apartment block.

Zeb was circling the mansion, Rivera's voice coming through

his SUV's speakers, when the gang boss gave him the address.

His eyes flicked to the mirror.

There were a few lights behind him, none too close.

He slid down his window, reached out to the passenger seat and withdrew a device he was very familiar with.

His gripped it in his left hand, waited for the right spot, where the foliage around the mansion thinned, and let fly.

The device was dark and blended against the sky. From behind, it would look like Zeb was stretching his arm.

Rivera was in the yard, checking on his men, making sure they were patrolling, their guard wasn't down, when the device landed inside.

Their eyes turned to follow it, watched it bounce once.

The next second, a thousand suns blazed and the accompanying explosion knocked them to the ground.

Half blind and deaf, his ears ringing, spots and colors dancing in front of his eyes, Rivera stumbled to his feet, reached out with his hands to hold onto something, anything, when the phone in his hand squawked.

'That was a flash bang.' Carter's voice sounded tinny, faded in and out. 'It was a warning. Stop looking for me.'

Hours later, with a shower and several hours of sleep behind him, Zeb drove through the Edison Park neighborhood. It was in the far Northwest Side and was one of the few neighborhoods in the city that had the least crime.

Named after the inventor, the community area had a large proportion of Irish ancestry, which was evident from the number of Irish bars, as he drove through.

Low crime. Not the kind of neighborhood people would associate with assassins.

The apartment block was a three-story building with six apartments facing the street, six others at the back of the block.

There was a small yard in the front in which a few kids played. Narrow alleys cut through the sides of the block, with a basement parking lot feeding into the alleys.

Ajdan's apartment was on the ground floor.

Makes sense. He will want easy exits.

The block had a gated entrance and during his first pass, he realized it would be difficult to breach the apartment.

Small community. Strangers will stand out.

123

In the second pass, he decided Ajdan's apartment was a dummy. The windows showed no signs of care, the curtains were dirty and the yard in front of the apartment was overgrown.

Probably one of their many addresses.

He circled the block a few more times and when the mail truck rolled in, the idea came to him.

It took him two days to organize the envelope. It had to be shipped from his office in New York. Broker or the twins would normally have dispatched it, if they had been around.

A friend in the NYPD, who had access to their office, arranged the shipment.

The envelope was like any other found in thousands of stationery stores across the country. It was thick, brown, and just larger than the size of a full sheet of paper, with an adhesive strip on its flap.

Its construction made it unique.

Embedded in the envelope was a network of near invisible filaments, wires, which ran the length and breadth of envelope. The bottom fold was padded and contained a small chip.

The envelope was a GPS tracker, the wires, its antenna.

Zeb printed a sheet of paper, inserted it in the envelope, and posted it.

The envelope got delivered the next day. It lay in the apartment's mailbox for two days.

On the third day a bicycle courier entered the block, grabbed the mail, stuffed it in his bag, and sped away.

Zeb followed him to Franklin Park where the mail changed hands. It got delivered to a business services office. One of those where you could rent an address and office space.

The mail remained there for just one day.

The business center put it in a larger package and couriered it to a cab company in Englewood.

A Chinese man picked the package, bundled it along with a local newspaper, and during his delivery rounds, had flung it in front of a brownstone on West Armitage Avenue in Lincoln Park.

This is more like it.

The homes on that street went for seven figures. The brownstone was the perfect cover for Ajdan.

He probably poses as a businessman.

Zeb nosed his Mercedes GLA into a tight space behind a BMW, settled down to wait. The Mercedes blended well with the other German and Italian make vehicles on the street. It even had plates similar to those of the other vehicles.

Its dark exterior gave him sufficient cover. It came with built in WiFi, which sealed the deal for him.

The package lay in the front yard till the evening, during which the brownstone's door didn't open once.

Zeb had a range of equipment beside him. A sniper rifle with Leupold scope, NVG, and helmet. A video and still camera that could shoot in day or night was mounted on a stand on the dash.

There was a red and blue flasher and police siren both of which operated on a timer. He set it.

In addition, there were two pieces of equipment that only the Agency and the NSA had access to.

One was a Doppler radar device that pinged structures and detected motion behind walls. It could sense the slightest motion such as breathing or the twitch of a limb. Its sensitivity and algorithms had been tweaked and fed to a holographic projector on his laptop.

Zeb had used the radar on several occasions in the Middle East; it hadn't let him down once.

The other device was an acoustic transducer that sent special frequency waves through metal walls and detected life behind it.

The street lamps came on and half an hour later, the brownstone's door opened, a dark-haired man emerged and picked up the bundle on the front yard.

The camera silently captured him.

Zeb didn't have to look twice to confirm this was the second assassin. The size fit, the posture was the same.

He turned his attention to the holographic projection.

The assassin shut the door behind him and walked to a structure, a table.

He tossed the bundle on it and was joined by another man.

Zeb moved swiftly. The mask went on his head. The Glock went in his holster. A shaped explosive charge capable of blowing down steel reinforced doors was in his right hand. Flash-bangs filled his pockets.

He swung the door open and a countdown began in his

mind.

Ten minutes.

He ran across the street, deserted in the growing dark, crossed the front yard swiftly, crouched below the peephole and attached the explosives.

Shiraz unwrapped the bundle, threw the newspaper away, went through flyers, leaflets, bills. Ajdan idly read a few, dumped them in a trash can beneath the table.

He picked a couple of bills, placed them aside. The utilities in the Edison Park apartment were paid directly through a bank account that was always topped up, but sometimes other bills crept in.

An assassin's life wasn't as automated as he wished.

Shiraz picked the brown folder, turned it around for a return address.

There wasn't one.

He shrugged, tore open the flap.

He frowned when he saw the single sheet of paper inside.

He extracted it and laid it on the table.

Ajdan crowded his shoulder and the two men read the single line.

THERE ARE NO RETIRED ASSASSINS. NOT YET.

Shiraz frowned. 'What does it mean? Who's it from?'

Ajdan was already moving when the loud wail tore through the silent street.

Cops.

He grabbed Shiraz by the shoulders, shoved him to the polished floor.

'It's him.'

He looked around desperately for his gun.

Too late!

The door splintered and fragmented, air got sucked out of the room. Lights went out, a blinding flash and an accompanying roar rent the air.

Ajdan was stunned momentarily, but he had trained for this; had experienced several live attacks.

All that experience and training came to good use. He shut his eyes tightly, gripped Shiraz with one hand and kicked out with his legs. They slid smoothly on the wooden floor, toward the hollow under the staircase.

Flashes stabbed, rounds thudded in the walls behind them

and then they were falling.

Eight minutes.

Zeb spotted the figures, once the incandescent light died away, blobs on his NVGS, one of whom was already moving.

He aimed, shot, knew he had missed, but continued firing, spraying the room with lethal rounds that spit through the air with their narrow channels.

The figures moved fast.

Floor's polished.

His gun followed them, spit flame, but then they were falling and disappeared out of sight.

He kept a steady stream of fire, changing mags automatically, his hands blurring without conscious thought, as he approached where they had disappeared.

Crawl space, he thought initially when he saw the well beneath the steps.

No, it's an escape route.

The small square of space, three by three feet, now empty, was cunningly built beneath the stairs that led to the second floor.

The tapering slope of the stairwell came to an end just before it met the ground floor and became a vertical wall.

Not a wall. A concrete door.

He emptied a magazine in the wall.

Chips flew, white dust filled the air, but the rounds didn't go through.

Probably more than a foot thick.

He hopped inside the well cautiously and studied the wall. Only the barely visible cracks on the four sides gave it away as a door.

Probably hinges from inside, motorized mechanism and lock.

He pushed, pulled, searched for hidden levers. He found none.

Seven minutes.

He dug into his pockets, dug out a shaped charge, stuck it to the door, and rigged a trigger that would blow the charge when the door opened.

He climbed back to the ground floor, searched the rooms thoroughly, living room first, then the diner and kitchen.

He didn't find it.

He climbed the stairs, Glock pointing ahead, paused for a second on the landing.

The landing opened into two bedrooms, a bathroom, and a study.

The first bedroom, the smaller one, was neatly made out, but didn't have anything of interest to him.

The study had a metal desk and a swivel chair. The desk's surface was bare. A chest of drawers hid a printer and papers.

No computers, no files.

Five minutes.

The largest bedroom had a router, a notebook, clothes, shoes, bags, dirty laundry. He looked under the bed. It was bare.

He slapped the pillows down.

There!

He tossed one of the pillows away and found a laptop.

Three minutes.

He searched for its power cable, didn't find one.

It's a standard make. You can buy one.

He hurried down the stairs, paused for a minute before exiting the house.

There were bystanders, dog walkers, people pointing cameras and phones.

He made sure his mask was donned, made his gun visible and ran to his SUV.

'Police. Stand back!'

They fell back, despite his mask. People usually looked at the whole, not the specifics; his demeanor and the voice of authority was enough for them to believe him. It helped when his command was backed by the flashers and the siren from his ride.

'Keep away from the house,' he ordered one last time and drove away.

An hour later he had swapped vehicles at a Walmart, changed clothes, and was now dressed in a brown jacket, a thin moustache, and shades. The laptop now had a power cable.

He turned on the radio, switched stations till he found a news channel and heard reports about an attack on a suburban home in Lincoln Park.

The police were hunting for a masked man posing as a cop.

He was armed and dangerous and residents of the city were asked to stay away from him.

No bodies had been found at the house. An explosive device had been rendered harmless.

'Terrorists,' the news reporter answered the studio anchor's question.

The terrorist drove his vehicle to O'Hare, sticking to the speed limit, acting normally. He passed several cruisers that raced by with lights flashing. Not one of them glanced in his direction.

He was confident he hadn't left behind anything at the house.

Grabbing the assassins or killing them had never been his objective. That would have been easier achieved by tipping Burke off and getting the FBI's HRT involved.

The Fed's Hostage Rescue Teams were professionals and would have taken down the assassins, but not without encountering stiff resistance.

Even if captured, they would have taken a long time to reveal anything. If at all.

Nope, it was better this way. Shock them with a surprise attack. Give the impression of a large police force. Give no time to assess or react. Let them escape.

It was the laptop that was important.

Assassins such as Ajdan were paid to kill.

He wanted to know who had paid them.

The paymaster would have the answers.

Chapter 15

The paymaster, Boiler, was being massaged in Florida, in his beach house. The masseuse was a stone-faced Cuban woman who silently dug her fingers hard in the shoulders of her client.

Surf pounded in the near distance, laughter and chatter of families, holiday makers, came through the walls of the house. The Florida sun shone brightly on blue waters; golden sand and tanned bodies bathed in its warmth.

Boiler heard and saw none of that.

He was listening to an update from his man.

He had sent a two-man team to check out the fourteen remaining men.

The plan was for his two gangbangers to shadow each of the men for about a week, till they were sure that he was or wasn't Cezar. Both the men knew Cezar and his woman well.

If the man wasn't Cezar, they would move to the next town and the next man.

His team had crossed out four men so far. They had started in North Carolina and had moved to Virginia, Maryland, and were now in Pennsylvania.

Checking out small towns, just like how the Marshals' mole had said.

No luck so far.

His men communicated regularly to one of Boiler's hoods who briefed Boiler as soon as there was anything relevant.

Boiler waved him away when he had finished.

The masseuse tapped him on his left shoulder. He grunted, moved up on the bed and she started on his lower back.

He snapped his fingers. Another hood stepped in.

He gave a break down on Chicago.

Boiler knew about Carter's attack on Ajdan and that Ajdan and Shiraz had escaped just in time.

Ajdan had communicated with him briefly once he had holed up in a new hideout.

The Armenian's hacker had given up trying to find anything in Carter's past. Both Ajdan and Boiler had independently surmised that the Carter and Parker had some shared army history.

'He seems to have given us an out.'

Boiler listened while Ajdan explained the note. 'None of

those rounds came close to us. We were sitting ducks. He could've taken us out.'

'What was he after?'

Ajdan took a deep breath. 'He got my laptop.'

Boiler knew it was encrypted, but so far Carter had proved to be resourceful.

He would eventually find out Ajdan's connection to Boiler.

Boiler didn't waste energy on recrimination. Ajdan and he had been through a lot together.

'Find him before he finds all of us.'

Milton Mills knew that Zeb was back when Olivia Wade spotted him returning from his early morning run.

She dashed down to tell her mom who listened distractedly while she got her breakfast ready.

Jenny Wade taught in the local school and also worked part-time in the post office. 'Get dressed, honey. Mr. Carter will be here for a few days, I guess.'

Olivia scrunched her face in disgust at her mom's indifference and ran upstairs.

She had spoken to Mr. Carter. She knew his first name. Not a single other person in the village had got that far.

She peeked through her window that looked into his backyard. It was empty. She stared at the glass door in the rear, willing him to appear, but he didn't.

She reluctantly turned away when her mom called from beneath, urging her to get ready.

She hurried when it struck her that she was the only one who knew of his arrival. It would be hot news in school.

Late that evening, Jenny Wade stood in her daughter's bedroom and glanced at her neighbor's backyard.

It was dimly lit, light from the inside leaking through the rear door, turning dark to pale yellow.

Olivia endlessly speculated on who he was, what he did.

'Maybe he's a firefighter,' she had exclaimed. 'Or a cop.'

'Honey, he might just be a banker, or maybe he works in some government office.'

Olivia had shaken her head forcefully, her blond curls flying around. 'Not even close, Mommy.'

Jenny straightened the blanket over her sleeping daughter and stroked her hair tenderly.

She was inclined to agree with Livy. Mr. Carter didn't look like a banker or like someone holding down an office job. He was a fixture now, but the gossip about him hadn't died down.

She massaged Livy's feet, remembered a time when she had come up to her daughter's room to hear strange sounds.

She had peered cautiously and had gaped at the sight.

Livy was in a boxing stance, no not boxing, a martial arts stance, her tiny hands flailing, her legs rising to kick invisible opponents.

Jenny had followed her eyes and what she saw had made her go still.

Mr. Carter was in his backyard, bare-chested, lightly covered in a thin sheen of sweat.

His head was still, just his hands and feet moving in complicated motions, strikes and parries, reaching out, drawing back, in waves, slow, fast, slow, fast, till they blurred in motion.

He had stopped after a few minutes and had bent to sip from a bottle of water.

She had sucked in her breath when she saw his back. There were scars. Pock marks.

She had seen such marks before, on someone else, in a different lifetime. They were scars. Bullet wounds.

She saw Mr. Carter - she, and in fact the entire village called him by that name - when she was driving out to school the next day.

He was hauling boxes through his front door, nodded at her when she waved, and then she lost sight of him.

They had never spoken even though she and he had been the only two patrons in a restaurant in Milton once. He had sat in a corner having his dinner while she was being served.

That evening was fresh in her memory even though it was more than a year back.

The waitress had been a young girl who was a student in Jenny's school.

Midway through their meal, a couple of men had come in, high on something, maybe alcohol, or on life itself.

They behaved the way young men sometimes did. Talking loudly, looking around carelessly, making comments about women.

The waitress served them, smiled gamely when one of them

133

said something to her while the other man laughed.

She came back with their order and this time she left iron-faced.

The men didn't let up. One of them signaled her.

She moved reluctantly, took his order, returned with their drinks.

Jenny didn't see what happened. Something must have, a hand must have groped or tried to, because the girl moved back suddenly, her face flamed, the men laughed.

Jenny rose, but before she could take a step, Mr. Carter had moved.

He brought his plate, his glass, and seated himself at the table opposite them.

He didn't say a word. He dug into his meal and ate slowly. Looked at nothing in particular.

The men's laughter dialed down a notch.

Not for long.

A hand waved. The waitress didn't move.

One of the men called out loudly.

She came reluctantly, stood at a distance, her pad ready.

This time Mr. Carter raised his head.

He looked at the men directly and something happened.

Jenny Wade would swear to herself later that he didn't speak, he didn't move a muscle and yet the men seemed to shrink.

Their voices lowered, they became polite.

They left shortly without looking back.

Jenny had spoken to the waitress the next day. She had felt *something*, but couldn't describe it. All she knew was that Mr. Carter's presence had tamed the men.

Jenny spoke about the incident to Pike, who brought it out every time Mr. Carter's name came up in conversation.

Jenny Wade shook her head to clear her thoughts and drove into the school's parking lot.

Zeb tightened the nylon ropes outside his home and tested them.

The ropes ran from the roof to the ground where they were knotted securely in steel hooks. The ropes were white in color and blended against the exterior of the home.

They didn't look it, but each one could bear thousands of pounds in weight.

Their tautness ensured they didn't sway with the breeze and were visible only if someone stood really close to the house. Fifty such ropes circled the home and at least a couple were in easy access from each window.

Decoration. That would be his answer if anyone asked. No one had.

He looked up and down. No one was in sight.

He went inside to a bedroom window, swung a leg over the sill, gripped one rope in his left hand, swung his body out, slid quickly, reached out with his right and swung over to the next rope.

He repeated the maneuver several times till he got it right.

Not quite Tarzan, but he was getting there.

He could exit from one window at the top, in the front, and could swing around and enter the house from a rear window.

He dusted his hands and looked back at his day's work before heading inside.

One never knew when a fast escape would be required.

Sarah Burke was fuming. Her task force knew it, kept their distance from her. Even Mark Kowalski, who was the closest to her, stayed in his cubicle.

They had pursued the leads Carter had given them but hadn't gone far with those.

They had gone back to basics and had run a grid search for CCTV camera images in Chicago. Had run a facial recognition program that compared the assassins' photographs Carter had given them.

That had narrowed down the images to fifty possibles.

Good detective work – digging out identities, making calls, checking travel records, financial records – had narrowed that down to fifteen.

One of those possibles was a brownstone in Lincoln Park.

Burke had wanted to mount surveillance. She had organized the teams and was readying to send them when Kowalski came running to her, pointed to a TV.

The brownstone was trashed; its occupants were missing.

Which was why she was fuming.

Carter. Who else could it have been?

She called Chicago P.D., got more info, read the reports that came to her a few minutes later and mussed her carefully styled hair.

At the least, I can get him for impersonating the police.

A second later, she deflated.

Yeah? Who's going to back you up, Burke? Director Murphy? He's best buddies with Carter.

She exited her cubicle, ignored the ducking motions by her crew, went to the water cooler and drank deeply. She had water bottles on her desk, but she needed the motion or else she would scream and throw something.

Special Agent Sarah Burke didn't scream. Not in front of her crew.

It was while she was applying wet fingers to her temple that Director Murphy appeared in the corridor, talking animatedly to a woman.

Burke couldn't help noticing the woman. She was tall, maybe five eleven, with fine features, but it was her eyes that held Burke's attention.

They were grey ice. Cool, sharp, a cutting edge to them.

They approached Burke who stood aside to let them pass.

They didn't.

Director Murphy stopped and introduced her to the woman.

'Clare, meet Special Agent in Charge, Sarah Burke. She's not only our ace investigator, she also heads the task force that's investigating the Parker murders and all those related to it.'

Burke felt she was being read, the way the grey eyes probed her.

'You are the one who almost pulled a gun on Zeb?' The woman asked with a slight smile.

Zeb, not Carter.

'You know him, ma'am?'

Clare inclined her head. 'Very well.'

'In that case, could you ask him to co-operate, please?' She didn't care that her tone was abrupt. She had enough of the kid glove treatment meted out to Carter.

Clare's smile grew wider. 'He is,' and with that she walked away with the director.

Burke dug her nails in her palms, closed her eyes, flashed them open when Kowalski tapped her shoulder.

'I think you should see this.'

He led her to her cubicle that now had a package on her desk.

It was the size of a briefcase, heavy, and was addressed to

her. It had no return address.

She sliced it open, her crew crowding behind her, removed the bubble wrap and removed a laptop.

She studied it for a second before flipping it open.

A sheet of paper covered the keyboard.

She lifted the sheet and saw that it had an address on it.

The brownstone's address.

Lambo and Diesel, Boiler's two-man crew had covered several hundred miles in their Toyota Land Cruiser.

It was silver and shiny when they had left Chicago, but was now scratched, dented, and the shine had faded to a dull gleam.

Lambo and Diesel were tired and cranky. They had covered twelve towns, now only two remained.

They had spoken briefly to Boiler. He wasn't happy, but there was nothing they could do.

It was not as if they could produce Cezar out of thin air.

Diesel spread a map on the hood, at a rest stop on the outskirts of Connecticut and traced their route.

Lambo stifled a yawn and nodded. His attention lingered on a woman who walked by. He watched the way her jeans stretched over her bottom, nudged Diesel and the two of them stared hungrily.

Damn. It had been a long time since they both had women.

Boiler's commands had been explicit however. They had to remain clean, not draw attention to themselves.

Lambo hauled his ass in the driver's seat once the woman disappeared and floored it.

Connecticut.

If Cezar wasn't there, then the last town.

Brookfield in New Hampshire.

Chapter 16

Union, in Connecticut, population close to nine hundred, was a waste of time.

Diesel came close to capping the gas station owner when he laughed, showing blackened teeth. 'Diesel? What kind of name is that?'

Diesel smiled politely, paid him and left before he rearranged the man's face.

Polite. Boiler had told them to smile a lot and be polite.

It wasn't easy. But if one wanted to recover thirty million, some changes in behavior were necessary.

Lambo and Diesel spent three days in Union before giving up. They drove through the entire town, which didn't take a lot of time, spoke to people, mentioned their cover of buying a retirement home for their folks.

They bought a lot of drinks.

Zip. Nada. Cezar wasn't here.

Diesel brought out the map again, which was coming apart at the folds by now.

He scratched his ass, put a dirty nail on Union and dragged it to Brookfield.

'Toll roads on the way.'

'Screw that,' Lambo flared. 'Boiler won't pay us back, besides they have cameras at the booths. Let's go the longer route. It's not as if we are working to a timeline.'

They were.

Big G was becoming impatient. Boiler told him to stay put, he was handling it. Big G knew that, but if Boiler didn't find Cezar soon, he, Big G, would break out of prison and lead the hunt himself.

He had it all planned out. He knew which prison officers to bribe, how the escape would happen, who would rendezvous with him, everything, down to the getaway vehicle and the flight from Mexico, was in his mind.

Boiler protested.

Big G escaping would bring unwanted scrutiny on the gang.

He didn't mention that Big G was unstable and would likely leave a blood trail across the country, a blood trail that would bring down the Feds on all of them.

He did mention that Cezar would change identities yet

again, once Big G's escape flashed on TV screens all over the country.

That was the clincher for Big G.

He calmed down. But then he gave Boiler a deadline.

One month. If Cezar wasn't found in one month, Big G would hunt him down.

Lambo and Diesel got lost.

In trying to avoid toll roads, Diesel took small country roads that wound through acres of fields and valleys and hills.

Lambo's phone died and he had lost his charger along the way; Diesel's phone didn't have a maps program on it and that worsened matters.

By the time they saw a signboard, they were hungry, tired, and grumpy.

'Milton Mills,' Lambo read aloud. 'I saw this on the map. Place has got like three hundred folks in it.'

'How far is it from Brookfield?'

Lambo shrugged. 'Let's grab a bite, rest our asses, and then we'll figure it out.'

Chuck was loading barrels of beer beneath the bar when the strangers drove up. He heard the sound of the engine first and frowned. It was early, barely ten in the morning, the bar normally started filling up around noon.

He rose from behind the bar; saw the silver SUV back up into a parking space. Two men stepped out, adjusted their belts, and stepped in the direction of the entrance.

They entered seconds later and while one of them headed to the john, the other ambled across to him, scanned the menu and placed an order for hash browns and coffee.

Strangers weren't uncommon in the village and Chuck took no notice of them till one of them asked if there were any houses for sale.

For sale meant buyers. Buyers meant money.

There weren't any homes for sale really, but that didn't stop Chuck giving the men a low down on the village. It was the first time he had spoken freely.

'You fellas be staying a few days?'

The older one, who said his name was Lambo, hesitated, wiped his mouth with a napkin, looked at his partner, and then replied.

'We've been looking at some towns for our boss to buy a home in. He's a big-shot attorney in New York who's always wanted to have a retirement home in a town like this. We were actually heading to Brookfield, but we got lost.'

Chuck felt opportunity slipping away. He made his pitch. 'Milton Mills is a great little village. You've got everything here. Quiet life. A river to paddle in. if you're boss hankers for the bright lights, then heck, Milton is just across the street.'

'Brookfield ain't got anything on our village,' he snorted.

Lambo held a palm up in acceptance. 'You've sold us. We'll stay a few days, make a list, send our report and then move onto Brookfield. After that it's outta our hands.'

Chuck nodded sagely as if he knew how these deals went down.

'You'll find me here in case you need more information.'

Lambo grinned. 'We might take you up on that. Say, can you give us a rundown on who stays here? The residents? The boss likes to get a feel for his neighbors.'

Chuck went behind the bar, grabbed a pot of coffee, poured three cups, hauled a chair for himself and began.

'Why did you say we'd stay here?' Diesel hissed at Lambo.

'Anything to get him off our backs.'

Diesel watched the bartender go about his business, polishing glasses, arranging them in pegs behind him. 'We might as well rest for a day here. Brookfield ain't going anywhere.'

Lambo raised a glass to that. 'My ass feels like a car seat. It needs to fill out again.'

They had mapped out the village by the second day, knew almost every resident by sight and were spending big money, by the village's standards, in Chuck's bar.

They went to the post office the third day, parked outside, enjoyed the fading sun for a few moments and then went inside.

Lambo had bought a map earlier, along with an envelope and some picture postcards. He addressed the envelope, placed the postcards in it, sealed it and went to the window.

The blonde behind the glass smiled at him, took the envelope and stamped it. She took his money, returned his change, and looked behind him for the next customer.

There wasn't anyone behind him. Diesel had been crowding

him earlier, but he had walked out.

His partner had the engine running and floored it the second Lambo seated himself.

He drove fast, without saying a word and it was only at the motel that he uttered his first words.

'She recognize you?'

'Who?' Lambo asked stupidly.

Diesel took in the bewilderment on his partner's face, dug out his jacket and removed one photograph.

He tapped it. 'That's Cezar's woman.'

Lambo stared and then stared again.

Cezar's woman was the lady behind the glass.

In Milton Mills. A town that had not been on their list.

Theo, the pony-tailed wizard in Burke's task force, took two days to crack the laptop. The security on it wasn't NSA standard, but it wasn't common garden variety either. Once his algorithms had done the job, the laptop opened its secrets to him.

The first task was to download the emails, zip them down to a manageable size and send them to Burke.

He then turned his attention to the IP addresses on the *From* and *To* emails. The addresses were hidden by proxies and no doubt were bounced from server to server.

Not a problem. He was the best proxy hunter the Feds had. He activated his sniffer programs and pulled up the browser's history. It was blank. The recycle bin was similarly empty.

They wouldn't be, for long.

Burke and Kowalski were in a meeting room with the rest of the task force, examining the emails.

The emails were initially baffling. One set was about commodity prices. Another set was about futures oil prices. Yet another lot was about currency exchange rates.

The assassin signed off with just an initial, *A,* and so did his recipients. Recipient. Most of the mails were between *A,* who Burke assumed to be Ajdan, and one other person, who too signed off with an initial, P.

'They are jobs, assignments,' Burke said suddenly. 'Each set of emails is about a specific job with his cutout, P. The commodity is irrelevant. The numbers next to them are either the price, or the timing of the hit.'

'You're onto something, boss,' Kowalski broke out excitedly. He typed furiously on his tablet. 'I'll search timelines and see what went down in those windows.'

Burke sifted through the printed sheets till she found emails before and after the Parker killings.

She hit a wall.

None of those mails had prices. They didn't refer to the Parker murder.

She dipped her fingers in a glass of water and applied them to her temples to ward off a migraine.

He didn't kill Parker? Or if he did, it wasn't routed through the cutout?

She decided to attack it from a different angle. *Assume that he killed Parker.*

'Run a CCTV image search in and around Damascus. Gas stations, motels, car rentals, airports. I want images from whatever has a lens.'

Kowalski bobbed his head in acknowledgement and spoke low in his phone.

The Patriot Act had made things easy for the FBI; with its backing, there was little that they couldn't grab. Emails, images, videos, files, records, nothing was beyond the reach of the Act, and what's more, it required none of the bureaucratic hassle of the pre-Act days.

Burke settled back, knowing she was close. She would crack this wide open. Ajdan might be the best contract killer out there, but Sarah Burke was the best the FBI had.

Ajdan wasn't taking new contracts.

His cutout had approached him with a lucrative assignment; to take out a Turkish general. The job paid well, extremely well, but he would have to travel outside the country.

He was wary of international travel. He didn't know to what extent his laptop had been compromised, but he had to assume that it had been.

Shiraz and he lived under a different cover now, in a different hideout, in Saint Paul, Minnesota. He was using a different communication protocol with his cutout.

He was still looking for Carter, but the man had disappeared and Ajdan didn't want to activate his usual intel channels. There was no knowing if those sources were now being monitored.

He went out one night, dressed in black, carrying just a

blade and his handgun, ignored the look Shiraz gave him and stepped in the dark.

He walked several blocks, to Frogtown, entered Western Avenue, a neighborhood known for its high crime rate.

He came across the drug dealers behind a block of housing for low-income families. There were three of them, hanging about with their low-riders almost to their knees, popping joints and shifting from foot to foot.

That time of the night, there was hardly any traffic. Maybe they were waiting for a trade to go down or a desperate buyer.

Ajdan didn't care. He watched them for a distance and when he was sure it was just them, with no other backup, he approached them.

His right hand went to the blade strapped to his thigh; even steps brought him closer to them.

One of them looked up, hearing his approach, muttered something to his companions.

They straightened, spread out and watched him come.

'You looking for a snort?'

Ajdan wasn't.

The blade slipped into his hand easily, flashed once in the dull light and got buried in the speaker's throat.

No warning, no talking, in the blink of an eye, one hood was down.

The blade came out smoothly, arced to the left and cut the second man's throat.

The third hood ran, a yell bubbling out of his throat.

He didn't get far.

Ajdan tripped him, yanked his head back and ruptured his lungs.

He wiped the blade on the dying hood's jacket, looked around and walked away.

He was a pro, one of the best assassins in the business. He only killed for hire.

However, sometimes the killing urge had to be answered.

Jenny Wade had a desperate urge to stop her car, jump out of it and snarl at the man following her.

Dade Joyner, thirty-eight years old, thought he was a gift to womankind. He had a tight, hard body, had his blond hair styled to his shoulders and had a ready laugh and a smile for women.

He had been through two wives; his womanizing had ended those marriages. He worked in a construction company and had made several passes at Jenny Wade when she had moved to the village.

She had rebuffed him, but Joyner didn't take refusal easily. He persisted and over the years, had turned downright nasty.

He followed her openly whenever he spotted her, brushed against her if they were in a store or in Chuck's bar, grinned and held his hands up in innocence when Jenny turned on him in a spitting rage.

She could have gone to the police, but she had her pride. She had Livy, who she didn't want to witness the interviews and the sheer hassle.

Joyner had turned up at the post office just as she was leaving, spotted her, broke away from wherever he was heading and leered at her.

She ignored him.

He followed her.

She quickened her steps and got in her car and swung away.

He pursued her in his.

She glanced once in the mirror. Joyner was stuck to her rear.

She had to go pick up Livy from school, go home, prepare dinner.

She took a slightly longer route to the school, hoping that Joyner would break away.

He didn't.

He parked behind her, was still there when she came out with Livy skipping beside her.

A bolt of panic shot through Jenny, but she swallowed it.

Milton Mills was a safe haven for her. Joyner wouldn't dare to approach her.

He stepped outside his car though and hogged the pavement, watching her insolently, his eyes running up and down her body.

She had to pass him to get to her car. She tried to skirt by, keeping as much distance as she could between them.

That wasn't enough.

'Stuck up, bitch.'

Her face flamed when she heard his low voice. She looked down once to see if Livy had heard.

Thankfully she hadn't. She was narrating her day at school.

Jenny picked up the pace, hustled her daughter to the car, opened her rear door and bent down to place Livy in her seat.

She saw Joyner's feet appear in the edge of her vision, then his legs, then his upper body.

Embarrassment and anger and fear flooded through her.

She knew what would happen.

Her skirt had tightened when she had bent.

Joyner would brush past her, *accidentally*.

She fumbled with seat belts, hurried, but Livy wasn't settling down.

She gave up, ducked out of the car, but it was too late.

Joyner was a just a foot away, his hip swinging toward her rear, his eyes burning hot.

Then he wasn't.

A wraith appeared beside him, a shadow.

It moved, became a person.

Its hand reached out, grabbed Joyner by the neck, dragged him back, and slammed his head on the roof of his car.

Joyner's lips split. His left cheek split. Blood flowed down his face, reddened the smart shirt he wore.

The shadow didn't let up.

It smashed his face again and only when Joyner had turned limp, the shadow let go.

Jenny Wade blinked, her mouth opening and closing, stumbling back.

It had happened so fast that her mind hadn't yet processed what her eyes had seen.

The shadow bent down and then her mind caught up.

Mr. Carter!

He bent over the moaning Joyner and said something. He rose, didn't glance at her, moved past her, buckled her daughter's seatbelt and then stood, one hand opening the door for her.

She moved in a daze, noticing but not really seeing his brown eyes. They were flat, impassive, and dark.

She slid in her car, turned the key and drove away, unthinkingly.

Later, much later, when her daughter had slept, when she had laced a rare cup of coffee with liquor, something came back to her.

Mr. Carter's words when he bent over Joyner.

'You can forget what happened, or you can go to the cops.

The choice is yours. Whatever you do, remember this. The next time you even come close to Ms. Wade, I'll break your legs.'

Dade Joyner didn't go to the cops.

He nursed his injuries, explained them as a bathroom accident, and hid his hurt and rage.

He spotted Carter a couple of times, thought about confronting him, attacking him at night, but when he felt those dark eyes on him, something moved in him. Something that was scared. Something that made him visit the restroom.

He nursed his anger and bitterness and hurt over drinks at Chuck's and that's where he met Lambo and Diesel.

They got talking, drinks were consumed, rage was ignored and temporarily forgotten when tales of women and their conquests came up.

He rose unsteadily an hour later, headed to the john, relieved himself and when he returned, he settled down with his new friends with a sigh.

His gaze moved in the bar and came upon a man in the corner. A man sitting alone.

Carter.

He cursed, caused his companions to look at him in astonishment.

Diesel thought Joyner had sworn at them and was prepared to do battle, when he saw the man's eyes were elsewhere.

His eyes followed and an involuntary sound escaped his mouth.

He nudged Lambo and directed his attention to the man in the corner.

He knew it for sure, when Lambo went still.

The man was Carter.

Carter and Cezar's woman were in the same town that hadn't been on their radar.

Boiler had to be informed.

Hunting You

Chapter 17

'Are you sure?' Boiler asked the same question he had asked before; it felt like years now.

Diesel's voice rose as he explained in elaborate detail. How they had seen her. Their following her, confirming where she worked, lived. Double checking with Chuck casually and other villagers.

'The timelines fit, boss.'

'There's no Cezar.' Boiler replied flatly.

'Nope. She came to town with just her girl.'

Boiler thought about it while he flipped through the photographs Diesel had sent to his phone.

He had passed them around to his crew and those who knew Cezar and his woman, confirmed that Jenny Wade was her.

Asking the snitch in the Marshals office was pointless. He didn't know any better.

'Boss?' Diesel's voice brought him back. 'About Carter –'

'He'll be handled,' Boiler cut him off.

'Boss, we should ask this Wade woman.'

'We will.' Boiler's face was a frightful sight to behold. 'We'll talk to her.'

He hung the phone up and called for Knuckles.

'We're leaving for Milton Mills.'

'Where's that?'

Boiler explained.

Knuckles' furrowed brow cleared. Going to some unheard of town, now made sense. 'When?'

'At the earliest.'

'Ten-man crew?'

Boiler drew out his blade and polished it unnecessarily. The knife was gleaming steel and could cut through flesh as if it was butter. He thought about crews and likely opposition.

The village was small and while the town of Milton had a police department, it wasn't big.

The plan was to hit the village like a gale, question Wade and disappear before any alarm could be raised.

It could be done. He had done it before. Several times. In several small towns in Florida and other states.

The villagers were mostly old. They wouldn't offer any opposition.

Carter? Maybe he was shacked up with Wade, though

Diesel said they lived separately.

Neighbors. They didn't interact, but that didn't mean anything.

Still, Carter was just one man.

Ten men should be enough.

'Twenty,' he ordered.

Burke stretched, stifled a yawn and rubbed the back of her neck. They had been poring through Theo's findings for twelve hours straight.

They had made progress.

A gas station near Damascus had a grainy image of a man who looked like Ajdan. He was accompanied by two men who looked like the other two assassins.

Theo had run the images through enhancement programs and was confident the three men were the killers.

The timing fit. The images were two days before the Parker killing.

Her crew was now chasing down motels in Damascus and the surrounding towns; the killers had to have spent the nights somewhere.

It was all coming together. Burke shared a rare high-five with her crew and ordered them back to their workstations.

She chewed her lip as her fingers stroked her phone.

Should I? He did send the laptop. Anonymously.

She fired off the text to Carter.

High probability that Ajdan killed Parker.

She didn't wait for a response. She knew none would be forthcoming. She turned her attention to printouts on her desk.

They had revealed other secrets.

They now had Ajdan's movements in the country. They had been able to crack several of the identities he used, and from there, it had been relatively easy to place him on the few flights he had taken, and at several car rental agencies.

They were also able to group his flights around possible hits in the country. A state government official in Kentucky. An oil company man in Texas. A lady chief executive in San Francisco.

There was just one flight a few years back that was seemingly unconnected to any killing.

A flight to Florida.

Kowalski and her crew had debated it for hours, but they

hadn't got anywhere.

She had a nagging feeling that flight was important.

She idly flicked through sheets on her desk. Reports from all over. Chicago P.D.'s reports on Churchey. On Carter.

Her hand stilled.

It went back to the report on Churchey.

Mobster. Chicago based.

But how about gangs in Florida?

Energized, she bent back to her laptop.

Moving twenty hoods from one part of the country to another wasn't easy.

Boiler decided to drive rather than fly. That was something he had learned from Ajdan.

Airports and train stations had clusters of cameras.

Cameras were bad for assassins and gangs.

He called one of their garages - they owned several - and asked for six SUVs to be readied.

All black, untraceable plates.

The garage acknowledged. The vehicles would be ready in two days.

He called Ajdan. The call was brief once they went through security protocols.

'Carter's in Milton Mills. So is Cezar's woman.'

He explained, not to any great length. Ajdan and he were similar in that respect. They didn't go in for lengthy, wordy conversations.

'Yes, we're sure,' he answered Ajdan's question and hung up.

They *were* sure, this time.

Lambo and Diesel had followed the Wade woman extensively and had videoed her. They had videoed Carter too.

His entire crew swore that Jenny Wade was Cezar's woman.

He conveyed one last message to a runner.

That runner passed the message to another courier in San Francisco. The Frisco guy spoke to a brother he knew in New Mexico, who knew a coyote.

A coyote was a people smuggler. Coyotes moved Mexicans and others from one side of the border to the other.

The movement was in one direction only. From Mexico to the United States.

The coyote moved the message down the line and it finally

reached Big G.

Cezar's woman has been located. Boiler is going after her.
Big G whooped in delight.

Zeb didn't get Burke's text.

He was kayaking in the Salmon Falls River, when his phone fell in the water. The phone that he used to communicate with Burke.

He thought of diving to retrieve it, but scrubbed the thought. He would contact her once he got back to the village.

In any case she needed time to piece together whatever was in the laptop.

He stretched back in satisfaction and looked up at the blue sky high above. The river was calm, silent, just like him. It had no other kayakers, which suited him just fine.

The river was life. For some, he was death, but the river understood him. It had run on its bed for hundreds of years. It knew all there was to know about life and death and good and bad.

Werner logged the text from Burke to Zeb. It paused its humming for a moment and sent the message to Broker and the rest of Zeb's crew.

Werner was bored. There was nothing on its plate that tasked it unduly. It flirted with supercomputers from around the world. There was one in Switzerland that it liked, but the Swiss Miss was yet to come online.

Werner yawned and stretched – the electronic equivalent – and was reading the latest research paper on quantum physics when the data packet came its way.

The data packet had a few words. Zeb Carter. Milton Mills.

Werner looked at the origins of the data packet. It came from a burner phone in Florida. It went to another burner phone in Minneapolis.

Werner logged the details and sent them to the crew.

It went back to the research paper. What its human masters did was up to them. Werner didn't understand humans. They had none of the binary logic that it had.

No wonder they're an inferior species, it sniffed.

The man in Mexico woke when his phone buzzed. He had different notifications for various people and this buzz, at two a.m. meant it was something important.

He rose, bare-chested, checked his message, logged onto his tablet and ran a few queries.

He stared out into the Mexican night, while waiting for the results to come in, seeing nothing, hearing nothing.

The night sky saw a tall, blond man in his late forties, clean shaven, with a ready smile in his eyes.

The reply came and when Broker read it, he knew what he had to do.

Things had been quiet. For too long. It looked like they wouldn't be for much longer.

His friend, Zeb Carter, seemed to be heading into trouble. It didn't look like his friend was aware of the storm clouds; even if he was, it was unlikely he would call for help.

Zeb wasn't built like that. He didn't have a *call for help* gene.

In dark of the night, Broker smiled.

So what if he didn't ask for help?

He scrolled through his contacts and called Meghan. She, Beth, Bwana, and Roger weren't far from him. They were in the Michoacan forests, less than a hundred miles away from him.

The phone rang once and then a groggy voice came on. 'It'd better be good, Broker.'

She heard him out silently.

'What's the plan?'

'I'm heading out. My work's almost done here. You folks enjoy your vacation.'

'Like hell we will. We are coming too. Wait up, I'll rouse the others.'

She put him on hold before he could protest and when her voice came back, he could hear others in the background.

One voice became louder. Bwana. 'What's up, bro?'

Broker explained once again.

'Of course, we're coming with you.' His voice faded and Broker could hear him yelling. 'Hey Rog, pack up. Fun time's over. Or rather, it's just starting.'

His voice came back stronger. 'You told Bear and Chloe?'

'Not yet. Look, Bwana, you guys are on vacation. Why don't you guys carry on? Zeb hasn't even asked for any help.'

Bwana snorted. 'As if he's going to. That guy's stubborn as a mule.'

His tone lowered, became serious. 'We're in. That's not up for discussion.'

It became lighter. 'Besides, we've had enough of this place. Capping some badasses will be a welcome distraction.'

'What about the civilians with you?'

'We'll ship them out. They won't be happy, but thcy'vc had us to themselves for a long time. Some hoods need our love, now.'

There was a muffled sound and presently a Texan drawl came on. 'What's the story, dude?'

Broker ran through it again for the third time, this time for Roger. He discussed logistics – the Gulfstream would pick them up – and thcn madc his last call.

Bear picked up on the third ring. 'This is about Zeb, right?'

Broker chuckled silently.

Most folks took Bear and Bwana to be muscle and brawn. Only a handful of people knew that the two of them were members of Mensa. The crew wasn't just about brute force. Chloe devoured scientific research in her free time, while Roger could debate philosophy with the best.

Bear would've figured things out once he got Werner's message.

He heard Chloe's voice in the background. 'Tell him, we've booked our flights and will touch down tomorrow.'

'Hey, what about your vacation?' Broker protested.

'We were on the down leg in any case, and were planning to be in Kathmandu in two days' time. All we're doing is advancing our return schedule by a day.' Bear's grin could be heard in his voice. 'Does Zeb know?'

'Nope.'

'Keep it that way.'

Broker went to the picture windows in his hotel and looked out at the night sky of Mexico City. A solitary car drove through the empty street down below, its twin beams cutting yellow tunnels through dark.

Zeb never called for help, whatever the odds against him. He was the first to show up whenever any of them were in trouble.

This time Zeb wouldn't be alone.

The deadliest fighting men and women would range beside him.

Chapter 18

Zeb assembled a new phone for Burke only a day later. He went to the backyard while messages were loading; everything looked the same. His neighbor's house looked empty.

School, work.

Force of habit made him check his perimeter. He had a discreet security system installed in the house; hidden cameras, intrusion detection, he even had cameras and monitors on the roof. The system didn't show signs of entry.

It wouldn't. This was Milton Mills. Nothing much ever happened here, which was why he loved the place.

His taking down of Joyner would probably fuel gossip for years.

His phone stopped buzzing, reminding him of Burke.

There was only one message that had been sent repeatedly by her.

High probability that Ajdan killed Parker.

He had suspected it would be something like this. Having it confirmed settled deep inside him.

His eyes were bleak when they rose from the pale glow of the screen. They saw nothing. They saw everything.

They saw death and vengeance and redemption.

Broker couldn't go back to sleep, so he went to querying Werner. It was a few more hours to light and then he would board the Gulfstream to pick up the others.

Enough time to find out exactly what's going on.

He read the reports from Zeb and Burke, asked Werner to dump everything on Ajdan, Churchey, and Rivera.

Zeb's queries to Werner made him grin. The to and fro on Maximus made him laugh. That man would never learn.

Werner could understand natural language. It didn't need to be programmed with computer-speak. If Zeb had explained clearly in the first instance, Werner would have responded.

The reports left him unsatisfied. The crucial questions remained unanswered.

All this started when Zeb was spotted at Parker's residence. Why?

He agreed with Zeb's theory that Parker and the rest were mistaken identity kills. That still didn't answer the question.

His coffee percolator gurgled. He rose, poured the steaming brew and inhaled deeply.

Coffee and good friends. What more did one need?

His laptop's screen beckoned.

Look at this differently.

He asked Werner to track down the two phones.

Werner came back in a minute.

The one in Minneapolis was untraceable. A burner phone from a lot that had been stolen from a Walmart a year back.

The one in Florida was promising. It was from a Best Buy, but its location during the call was intriguing.

The phone had been in the Little Haiti area, a neighborhood that Broker knew wasn't the safest in the city.

That still didn't lead anywhere. Saint Paul wasn't a high crime city, but he still looked up crime reports before and after the call. A week's window, leading to and after.

Assaults, burglaries, car thefts.

Homicides.

He skimmed the list, turned back to the homicides.

There were four killings. One in the week before the call, three – on the same day, the following week.

The killing before, was a domestic dispute. The husband was in custody and had confessed.

The three other killings were still being investigated. Dealers, who had been slashed brutally, had bled to death.

No witnesses. There never were.

Something triggered in his mind.

The Parkers had been slashed. So had been the victim in New Jersey and the Beattys.

Coincidence?

It still didn't get him anywhere and he rose in irritation to refill his cup. He never drank it.

It overflowed and scalded his fingers, but he didn't feel it, his mind whirling with the sudden realization.

Of course, dumbass. You should have listened to it fully.

He wiped his hands on a towel, rushed back to his machine and brought up the voice segment that Werner had captured.

He hadn't listened to it before. He had acted on the names Werner had flagged.

He listened now and got two more names.

Cezar. Jenny Wade.

Nope, neither of those names had cropped up previously.

He searched for Jenny Wade first. The last name would throw back more results.

Jenny Wade was a school teacher in Milton Mills.

Broker looked up her picture from DMV records, looked her up in various databases that he could access. Illegally. The legal route took too much time and required too many sign-offs.

One daughter.

No husband. No boyfriend.

Her backstory went back only five years.

That was an *ah-ha* moment. How could a person just pop up in the world with no extensive background detail?

Broker shelved the thought, moved onto Cezar.

That was a bad search. Werner came back with too many results to make sense.

He sat back and watched the sky lighten.

Okay, how about Cezar and Parker.

Nope.

Cezar and Damascus.

Nothing

Cezar and Churchey. Cezar and Rivera. Cezar and Ajdan, Minneapolis, Saint Paul, Chicago.

Werner returned nothing relevant.

Cezar and Miami.

Werner came back with results, a lot of them. Bars, hairdressers, businesses, none of them that made any sense to Broker.

On the third page of the results, he found a thread.

It was an extract from a newspaper.

Drug dealer turns informant.

Broker clicked on the link, looked up the date. It was seven years back.

He skimmed through the article; a dealer turned informant in Miami's largest criminal gang had spilled everything he knew, in return for protection. His intel led to the gang boss's eventual arrest in Mexico, where he was enjoying the government's hospitality.

Big G. *Where do these guys come up with these names?*

The story didn't mention Cezar, didn't have names. However, another article, a couple of years before the informer story, had Cezar in it. The drug dealer had been arrested for trafficking and had been bailed out.

Broker leaned back, laced his hands behind his head, closed his eyes and thought furiously.

Could Cezar be the informant?

He got Werner to run more searches, map patterns, use different algorithms.

Werner said yeah, there was a good probability. Cezar hadn't been heard of again after the informant story. No dead body matching his description had turned up, either.

Broker researched Big G's gang. He consumed megabytes of data on him, read about his rise to head one of the largest gangs in the country.

This is one dude who needed putting away.

How are Cezar, Jenny Wade and Zeb Carter connected?

Unless ....

A few more searches, hacking into some more secure, government databases, gave Broker some answers.

Not all of them. There were still some big holes missing. But what he had was enough, to justify calling the crew together.

He called up a tracking program, the one that kept tabs on all of them.

Zeb was still in Milton Mills. He had been on the river and was now back home.

Broker's fingers flew on the keyboard, buttons got punched and thousands of miles above, where there were billions of square miles of nothing, three satellites turned and pointed their extremely high resolution cameras at Milton Mills.

The satellites were part of Third Eye, a super-secret deployment of satellites that gave near real time feed to a couple of covert intelligence agencies in the country.

Agencies that the average citizen wasn't aware of. The average citizen didn't know of Third Eye either.

The satellites used heat signatures, lasers, radars, a dizzying array of technology that even Bwana and Bear couldn't fully grasp, which delivered video and images that had enabled several terrorists to be taken, remotely, off the table.

Broker had access to the satellites. Legally.

He overlaid the video feed with Zeb's GPS signal that came off the tracker in his shoes.

Now he had eyes on his friend.

There was one last task to be done before he showered and headed out to pick his friends up.

He sent a message to Zeb.

Zero.

Zero was readiness. It was the time before action. It was when vision sharpened, breathing slowed, everything became slo-mo.

Zero was when Zeb became time.

Burke was behind the curve. Well behind.

She didn't have access to the voice packet.

The Patriot Act gave her a lot of muscle, but listening to in-country conversations wasn't part of the deal. Another agency did that, but that agency and the FBI didn't always share.

However, she went with what she had to Pierce and Director Murphy. To get them to seek the other agency's help. Perhaps it had something on Ajdan.

Pierce and Murphy heard her out and then Pierce left them at a barely perceptible gesture from the director, who then punched a number and a phone rang at the other end.

It got picked up on the first ring.

A woman's voice came on the speakerphone.

Burke recognized it immediately.

It was Cool Grey-Eyed Lady, Clare.

'Pat, what can I do for you?'

Director Murphy nudged a shoulder at Burke. 'Tell her.'

Burke told her.

The director and Clare spoke for a minute, used terms that Burke didn't understand. Director Murphy smiled when the call ended. 'You'll get whatever the NSA has on these assassins.'

Burke fist-pumped mentally, thanked the director gravely, but couldn't keep the excitement out of her voice.

Even with that, she was behind the curve.

The first SUV came in the evening. It carried Knuckles and four other hoods. All of them were as neatly turned out as they could. Loose shirts over jeans or trousers. Jackets. Hair trimmed.

Boiler had been explicit. Try not to look like hoods.

They tried, but the best grooming couldn't conceal their disposition, the watchful eyes.

However, in the dark, there was no one to pick up on that air.

Knuckles lead the way to their motel. They checked in and

159

waited for the others to arrive.

By midnight, Milton Mills had twenty more residents, all of them housed in two motels less than a mile from the school, a mile and a half from Jenny Wade's house.

Diesel and Lambo met Boiler and Knuckles outside one motel and gave them the breakdown of the village.

'She's close to Chuck, the bar owner and Pike and Bundy. Sometimes Pike or Bundy delivers food to her, from the bar.'

Boiler gave instructions.

Five men would take the bar over.

Ten men would patrol the village and set a perimeter.

He, Knuckles, and three others would interrogate Jenny Wade.

'What of her girl?'

'Kill her. But only after we've finished with Wade.'

It wouldn't take more than two hours.

Two hours the next night, which was a Friday night.

Friday night, since the day after was Saturday and Jenny Wade didn't need to go to school.

Not that she would go, ever.

The next day, Zeb made calls, read, queried Werner, came close to calling Broker for help, but didn't. He didn't check his other phone. The one he used for his crew.

It's personal. Nothing to do with my team.

The problem was Ajdan had disappeared. Burke had no clue where he was. Chicago P.D. had no information.

Werner could have told him, but Zeb wasn't asking it the right questions.

Werner had sent him the message from the data packet, but Zeb had deleted it, unaware, while he was loading the phone for Burke.

Zeb was out of the loop while the threat vectors moved in his direction.

He went to Chuck's bar at mid-day, thinking about the Armenians, and paid scant notice to the three men in one corner.

Joyner, Diesel, and Lambo.

He finished his meal, smiled briefly at a joke from Pike, and left.

He checked his phone again. No new message from Burke. No news about Ajdan.

He unloaded the kayak from its trailer, polished it, made minor repairs, strapped the paddles in it, and when it had grown dark and street lights had come on, shouldered it into his garage.

He wouldn't need it for some time.

Till the business with Ajdan was resolved.

He turned out the lights in the garage, stepped out in his backyard and entered his house from the rear.

It was dark.

He rarely turned on lights and when he did, it was just the one in whichever room he occupied.

He wiped his shoes on the doormat, shut the glass sliding door behind him and walked up the stairs to the upper floor.

He entered his bedroom and tossed his phone on his bed.

His hands went to his waist, to remove his T-shirt and head to the shower, when he felt it.

Something in the way the still air wasn't still.

Hunting You

Chapter 19

Zeb moved.

Instinctively, without thinking, reflexes honed razor sharp, from years of combat and training.

He stepped back, a long step, and drew the Benchmade from its thigh sheath, all one motion, the steel flowing like silver liquid, muscles lubricated by adrenaline.

The blade came up, sliced through the wire that was stretching over his neck. Its upward motion turned to a sideways and downward swing.

Zeb ducked low, reached far behind him and the felt the point enter hard flesh with an accompanying hiss of breath.

He was turning to thrust again when another change in the stillness warned him.

He threw himself down, rolling fast, towards the window.

Just in time.

Three muted sounds, like books falling on a floor. A continuous roll, not separate trigger breaks.

A pro.

To my left and behind me. One man to garrotte me. Another to cover and shoot.

He counted the moves in his mind, the moves the shooter would make.

Stop firing. Track me. Resume.

On the third count, he rose, took one step and hurled himself out of the front facing window.

Glass splintered and gave way. Two more rounds tried to stop him, met air and darkness and went their solitary ways.

Ajdan shifted immediately, his Sig Sauer pointing straight and steady.

There wasn't anyone to aim at. Carter had vanished in the night.

He didn't relax. He searched the dark with his eyes, his ears tuned for the faintest sound.

Far away, in the distance, he heard engines and doors slamming.

Those sounds couldn't have been made by Carter. He couldn't have gone that far so quickly.

'How bad is it?' He asked in a low voice.

'Left abdomen punctured. Not deep. Will hold for some

time.'

Ajdan didn't feel rage or bitterness. He had stamped those emotions out a long while back. His friend would make it or he wouldn't.

There wasn't certainty in their business.

For now, they had to shut down Carter.

He approached the window, hugged a sidewall and peered out cautiously.

The night peered back at him.

Shiraz came from behind, handed him a small mirror.

Ajdan angled the mirror to see outside.

Exterior white walls came into view. The front yard. Pavement.

No Carter.

He shrugged at Shiraz's questioning look. His eyes flicked momentarily downwards, saw the spreading dark stain on his partner's body suit.

They had to finish this quickly.

'Let's secure the house. It might be a trap.'

The two flanked each other, covered one another and moved.

Shiraz in front. Ajdan behind. Their guns ready.

Chuck's bar wasn't difficult to take down.

Chuck, Pike, and Bundy were huddled together at the bar, an older couple was at a corner table, and a solitary man was at another.

Kadin entered the bar, his four men following him, took in the occupants and stepped to the left.

One man shut the door behind him.

Another went to the rear exit – the service exit – and shut it.

Chuck stared open mouthed for a moment and then yelled. 'Hey, buddy? What's up? Why're you closing the exits?'

Pike and Bundy echoed his questions.

Kadin walked over and gave him the eye. 'We're shutting you down for some time.'

Chuck opened his mouth to protest, Pike and Bundy rose, became voluble.

All three subsided when Kadin removed his handgun and placed it on the counter.

'This doesn't need to hurt.'

One hood went to the other occupants, took their phones

and placed them on the counter.

Kadin held his hand out at Chuck.

Chuck didn't move. 'Who're you guys? What's going down? You know the cops are just a couple of streets away.'

Kadin sighed, grabbed the gun and brought its barrel down on Chuck's forehead.

They didn't get any more resistance.

His men herded the occupants, took them down to the cellar and locked them in.

Four hoods stayed inside, one went outside to patrol.

Chuck's bar was now Boiler's.

Kadin pulled out his phone. 'Secure,' he said and hung up.

Secure. Just like in the movies. Heck, this was better than any flick.

Zeb flung himself sideways, air rushing past him, his left hand reaching out desperately.

It missed one rope, found the second. Fingers closed around it, grip tightened.

His body's swing turned. It headed back to the house. To a white wall. At collision speed.

His legs shot out, his knees braced and absorbed most of the impact. His head still jarred and if his teeth hadn't been locked tight, his tongue would've been bitten off.

No time.

A leg shot out. A hand reached out. Another rope was gripped.

He *ran* on the face of the house, rounded a corner, drew a deep breath and hauled himself to the roof.

He lay prone for several seconds, letting his pulse slow down, his breathing normalize, his night vision stabilize.

He rose, removed glass splinters from his shoulders and hair. One splinter, embedded in his right eyebrow, stubbornly refused to budge.

A stream of blood ran down his face when it did.

It'll stop. It's not blinding me.

He took stock.

His Benchmade was inside the house. All his weapons were inside. He was bare handed.

Weapons weren't a problem, however.

He went to the plastic water tank, bent beneath it and removed a cache from its underside.

Glock. Holster. Kevlar vest. Magazines. Another Benchmade. NVG. Blood blocker compress packs. Bandages. A stun grenade.

A cache that any self-respecting deep black operative would be proud of.

He suited and belted up.

Now to see where they are.

He went to a panel on the parapet and flipped it open. The recess would normally have fuses and switches for the house.

This one had all of those. It also had a screen on which feeds from the various cameras from within the house played.

The screen was powered by a long-life battery. So were the cameras inside.

The night vision cameras threw up the two hostiles as orange-yellow blobs.

They were fanning out, room to room, seeking him. Hunting him.

Ajdan and the other killer were in the second bedroom

Who else could it be?

How did they find me?

He scrubbed the thought. Now wasn't the time for *hows*.

They will be ready. Prepared. Coming from behind won't work. They may be prepared for the flash-bang.

The two blobs were now in the middle of the room. Two engines sounded, grew louder, faded.

He cocked his head. The village hardly saw traffic at night.

The blobs were exiting the second bedroom, were heading to the third.

He put the traffic out of his mind.

The third bedroom had a rear-facing window. It was open, to allow for air circulation.

A wild thought entered.

Can it be done?

What do I have to lose? I've practiced it. If it doesn't work, I'll try something else. So long as I'm outside, I'm good.

Thought became action.

He memorized the assassins' pace, their direction of travel, rose and headed to the parapet.

He slithered down a rope on the side of the house, braced his legs against the wall and stood perpendicular.

The rope, his body, the wall, a triangle.

The third bedroom window was ten feet away. The nylon

rope was long enough.

He reached down and slashed the rope beneath his legs.

His left hand twisted around the rope, his legs braced and then he was running on the wall.

Three steps, then airborne, flying out in an arc, like a pendulum.

The nylon taut and straight and turning into his hand and body, all stretched out in a thin dark line, flowing in the night.

Flying from one side of the house to the other.

Going over the window in the middle.

His right hand straightened, the Glock at its end. Its sight became larger in his vision.

The sight moved. Took in the fast moving wall. The edge of the window.

The darkness within.

Not darkness.

One shadow.

The shadow moved.

The sight moved.

His trigger finger moved.

Four shots pierced the night, punched through the darker shadow, and then he was out of sight.

His arc shortened. His flight dipped.

He landed; again vertical on the side of the house, bent his knees, and absorbed the shock.

His left hand moved of its own accord. Switched ropes.

The Glock got tucked away in his shoulder.

Right hand gripped the rope. Left hand followed.

He rolled over the parapet swiftly and headed to the screen.

One blob was down.

The other was in the first bedroom, from where he had escaped.

The blob looked at the camera. His gun came out. The camera went dark.

The second assassin, Ajdan, going by his height, shot out the rest of the cameras in the upper floor.

Zeb had no eyes in the house.

Not a problem. Now it's one on one.

Boiler checked with all his men.

All were accounted for.

The bar was in his control.

His men were patrolling the street.

Milton Mills was his.

He gestured at Lambo who floored the SUV and drove it to Jenny Wade's house.

The five of them spread out, moved swiftly down the paved walk, Boiler in the lead.

At the door, he stepped aside for Diesel to pick the lock. During their surveillance, they had found that the lock was basic.

It put up no resistance and gave way easily, the door swinging wide open for them to enter.

Boiler strode in. Passed the living room

Headed straight to the dining room where a light was burning.

It was late at night, but Jenny Wade was up, going through school work.

She felt the draft first, then heard the steps.

She looked up.

Her eyes widened in disbelief at the men ranging in front of her.

The first man had cold eyes. Green. His face was hard.

She recognized him. She had heard of him. She had wished never to see him. He was here now.

Her mouth widened, a scream came out.

'Olivia. RUN!'

Ajdan was sure Carter was on the roof.

He had, somehow, come off it and had shot Shiraz through the window. Four shots, three of which had caught his partner in his chest.

They both were wearing vests, but the fourth shot had caught Shiraz in the throat.

Four shots in less than ten seconds, within the narrowest window of opportunity.

Ajdan had underestimated Carter. This wasn't any ordinary soldier. This wasn't just any other special forces operative either.

There were probably a handful of men in the country who could make such shots count. Carter was one of those handful.

Get away.

That was Ajdan's priority now.

He lay face down on the landing and peered down the stairs. It was empty.

He strained his ears.

The house ticked, the refrigerator hummed. Somewhere outside, a door slammed.

No. Carter wasn't down below.

Ajdan would have sensed him.

He moved cautiously downstairs, crouching, making the smallest possible target, taking a step at a time.

Once he reached bottom, he changed positions swiftly.

No lance of flame came seeking his way.

The landing faced the kitchen. He had to go through it to get to the front door.

He took one step.

Another step.

The refrigerator came in sight. Dark. Tall. Gleaming in the night light.

A shadow moved on its surface.

Ajdan threw himself to the floor and fired a short burst in the direction of the shadow.

His rounds impacted something.

The wall.

Not human flesh.

'You killed Hank Parker.'

Ajdan didn't start at the voice. His gun didn't waver.

Carter's voice was normal, as if he was having a social conversation.

The voice came from the corner facing the refrigerator.

Ajdan tried to see through the darkness. He thought he saw a darker shape, but he had to be sure.

It could be a trap.

He moved stealthily, removed an empty magazine from his pocket and flung it at the shadow.

He rolled immediately to his left, his Sig rising to cover the shadow.

The magazine hit the wall and fell to the floor.

No human shape.

'You killed his family.'

The voice was behind him.

Ajdan dived away, poured a stream of lead at the voice, left to right, top to bottom.

Magazine change.

Gun ready.

He put his head to the floor, tried to see against its reflection.

A shadow moved, to the right of the voice.

Ajdan pushed away with his feet. Resisted the urge to fire.

He came to rest, eyes darting, ears keen.

His ears heard it first. The whisper of something moving in the air.

Like a limb.

He waited for the sound to repeat.

It didn't.

A twang sounded.

Crossbow!

He moved, but the arrow was faster.

It struck him in the right shoulder, embedded itself deep in his flesh.

His right side flamed in agony seconds later. His hand drooped. Sweat beaded his forehead.

He brought his gun hand up. Control mattered.

Anything was possible when he was in control.

The shadow moved again. This time he fired and dragged himself away.

Didn't empty his magazine, knowing the arrowed shoulder wouldn't allow a magazine change.

One round slapped something soft.

Triumph surged through him.

Flesh. Carter!

He raised his gun again.

And then again, heard the sickening twang.

The arrow went through him this time. Right through his left shoulder and exiting through his back.

What kind of arrow is that? He thought dimly, blinking his eyes fast, keeping perspiration away, trying to contain pain and rage and fear.

Trying to see through the night that seemed to have grown darker.

His gun was still up.

There was still hope.

The shadow moved again.

It came closer, became solid.

Became Carter.

He levelled his gun. It was feeling heavier by the minute.

Carter batted it away casually.

It flew, skittered on the floor and came to a stop.
Carter crouched.
His dark eyes bored holes in him.
'Hank Parker had my back.'
He moved.
The holes swallowed Ajdan.

Hunting You

Chapter 20

Chuck shuffled nervously in the cellar, his arms wrapped around his body to keep in the warmth.

The cellar stank of alcohol, old barrels, dampness, and sweat. It now also had the smell of fear.

The old couple sat tightly huddled in a corner, under the sole blanket in the corner.

The solitary man sat gazing vacantly at nothing, breaking his trance-like state to ask every now and then, 'Will we die?'

Chuck didn't know if they would die. Pike and Bundy came to him and stood silently, none of them knowing what to say.

The shock of their capture had worn off a long time back; then anger, argument, and debate had set in. When they realized escape was impossible, hope started leaking away silently.

Bundy moistened his lips. 'Who are they? I never saw them before? What do they want?'

He didn't get an answer. They didn't have any.

They listened, but the cellar walls were thick and other than own breathing in the small space, they heard nothing.

Time passed slowly, and it felt like an entire day had lapsed when they heard a step outside.

They rose as one, bunched together instinctively, the woman in their center.

Something at the thick wooden door rattled and it swung open.

Framed inside it was the biggest black man Chuck had seen. His eyes were flat, hard, cold, the assault rifle in his hand looked like a toy. He had tightly cropped hair, the muscles in his arms seemed to flex and ripple.

Behind him, another head appeared. Bearded, equally tall, a white man. He too had short hair, he too had the same air of menace.

Chuck drew around him the little dignity he had, clasped the hands of his friends and stood as straight as he could.

'Make it quick,' he said and hoped his voice didn't quaver.

The black man's eyes changed. He glanced once at the bearded man, turned back to the hostages.

'Make what quick?'

'You're going to kill us. Get it over with,' Pike snapped, his irascibility rising.

Black Man's eyes grew round. His face changed.

It relaxed; a smile grew on his face, so white and warm that something inside Chuck loosened despite the circumstances.

Black Man chuckled, started laughing, a rich sound that washed over them like a warm caress. Bearded Man grinned.

'Sir, no one's killing you. Not tonight.'

Livy had jumped out of her bed the moment she heard her mom scream. She had been disoriented for a second, but when her mom screamed again, she had hopped out of bed.

She knew what she had to do. Her mom had told her so many times, had made her do it for so often, that it became habit.

She breathed deeply, the way Mom had told her, tried to calm her thundering heart. She heard murmured noises from below, a sharp sound and a cry. Her mom's voice.

Her breath hitched. Her body trembled.

'LIVY, RUN!'

Her mom's voice came again and this time Livy moved automatically. She grabbed her teddy, raised the window, and was hitching a leg over the sill, when something stopped her.

She had to see. She had to know that Mom was okay.

Her heart was galloping faster than a horse, she felt like going to the bathroom, but Mom had told her she had to be brave if something happened. Mom had told her to go to Chuck's bar and stay there.

But she still had to see.

She turned back, crept to her door, slid it open and crawled to the stairwell. From there, she had a good view of the dining room.

Her breath choked. A sob escaped her.

Her mom was tied to a chair. Her lips were bleeding. Her thigh was bleeding.

A man came in front of her and stood there. A tall, bald man.

Livy bit her knuckles and tried to hold back her moan. It escaped her and at that, the man swung his face toward her.

Green eyes drilled her. The head nodded at someone and at that her paralysis broke.

With her mom's 'Run, Honey,' ringing in her ears, Livy fled.

She ran back to her room, shut the door and locked it.

She climbed over the window, leaned into the thick branch

of the tree that grew close to their window.

She hugged it for a second. Terrified of leaving her mom behind. Scared of going ahead.

Something crashed into her door.

She risked a glance behind. It still held.

A second crash propelled her forward on the branch. Her hands were clammy and started to slip, but she clung on somehow.

She knew she was sobbing, crying, and prayed that no one would hear her. She prayed that Mom would be okay.

She reached the trunk, slid down, the rough, cold, bark scraping her feet, her palms.

She tried to ignore the pain, tried to be brave.

But it was hard. That man was doing something to her mom. People were chasing her.

Her feet landed on ground, and after one last look at her bedroom window, she fled across the yard to the hedge separating their home from Mr. Carter's.

The hedge was thick and tall and impenetrable.

Except for a six-year-old girl.

Livy fell to her tummy and crawled beneath the barely-there gap that she and her mom had found.

Branches scraped her face, grass tickled her nose, mud dug into her nails and went into her mouth.

She was breathing loudly, panting, crying, and then she was in the small space, deep inside the hedge, invisible from the outside.

She sat up to draw a breath.

A hand clamped over her mouth.

Raul and Elbon were driving through the village, maintaining the perimeter. They were bored, hungry, but warm in the SUV.

Every now and then they checked in with Knuckles who was coordinating them.

'How long do we have to drive around, Knuckles?' Elbon grumbled.

'Till the bitch spills her guts.'

'Well, what's the holdup?'

A slap sounded, a scream followed.

Knuckles lowered his voice. 'You know how Boiler is. He likes to take his time. How's it out there?'

'This town's dead, man. Nothing's happening here.'

'Nothing will happen.' Knuckles said confidently. 'The bar's taken, Kadin's in charge. You guys sit tight. We'll be outta here, the moment Boiler does his thing.'

Elbon looked at Raul. 'You heard him. Boiler won't be rushed.'

Raul lowered the window and spat. He wiped his mouth with a hand and turned to retort when something on the road made him stop.

He stared. 'What the hell?'

A couple of women were outlined in their headlights.

Young, attractive, smiling as if they were in a bar, not on the road, in the dead of the night in Podunksville.

Elbon recovered swiftly. 'Check the sides, the rear. It might be a trap.'

Raul grabbed his gun, looked out and behind. 'No one this side.'

'Clear this end too.'

Elbon rolled to a stop near the women who shaded their eyes from the bright beams.

He lowered his window. 'What's up, ladies?'

'They're twins,' Raul murmured. 'Lookit the boobs on them.'

Elbon waved him to silence, poked his head out. 'You need a lift? Or something?'

He didn't see the shape emerge from behind him. He didn't feel an arm swing. Something that felt like a house, landed on him and then he felt nothing more. Raul swiveled in shock, grabbed his gun, and shoved his door open.

It slammed back, trapping his foot, twisting it. Before he could recover, a gun smashed into his mouth, and broke a couple of teeth.

A blond head came into his vision and smiled at him. 'He didn't put up much of a fight. What about you?'

The smile had no mirth in it, the eyes behind it were cold and then Raul joined Elbon.

Livy struggled, tried to scream, bit the hand covering her mouth, but the grip didn't let up.

Her sounds were muffled; her thrashing was subdued by an iron hand that pulled her little body tight against the man behind her.

Livy knew it was a man who had grabbed her. The body

was hard, even; the hands were like steel bands.

A man.

She was going to die. Her mom was going to die.

No sooner did the thought enter her mind than her thrashing increased. She kicked out with her small legs, slammed back with her head, but the man was unmoved.

He drew her back into a larger hole in the hedge that she didn't know existed.

Over her struggle, she heard shouting.

She stopped struggling, turned her head and what she saw sucked her breath away.

Two men were searching the backyard, their flashlights weaving back and forth, drawing oval shapes on the ground.

They were hunting her!

She froze, her blood pounded, she thought her heart might burst and come out of her body, it was pounding so hard.

The man behind her stood still, motionless, as if he was the hedge. It looked like he wasn't friends with them.

Livy took her cue from him, tried to stay motionless, prayed that the searchers couldn't hear her throbbing heart.

The men searched, one of them even looked under the hedge, but they gave up and went to the front of the house.

She thought the man would let her down now, would relax.

He didn't.

He stood without moving, his hold on her unyielding despite her resumed struggling.

His grip tightened and she sensed his head turn. She followed his gaze and saw the men had returned.

It was as if they had set a trap, waiting for her to emerge.

They searched the yard again, and this time, didn't return when they left.

The man still waited long minutes that felt like hours to Livy, then the steel bands around her loosened.

He placed her down and when she turned to face him, she started.

It was Mr. Carter.

She tried to tell him about her mom, the bad guys. The words didn't come. They were stuck in her throat.

She knew she was hypering, that word her mom used sometimes.

She tried to swallow. She choked and coughed.

She tried to speak again, but she started trembling, shivering, deep fear overpowering her. Tears leaking down her face.

Her mom would die. She had to tell him, but she couldn't.

Mr. Carter watched her for a second, then crouched and drew level with her.

He placed a hand on her shoulder.

It was warm. Solid. Firm.

It didn't tremble.

He looked into her eyes, as if reading her mind, as if knowing everything.

Livy started to relax. Her breathing became longer, deeper.

She licked her lips and tried again.

This time some words came. 'My mom,' she choked back a sob. 'Bad guys in the house.'

She knew they didn't make sense. She tried again, but the hyper thing started again and her words got stuck.

'How many?' Mr. Carter asked. His voice was gentle.

Livy shook her head. She didn't know.

A fresh river of tears started and somehow she shaped letters into words that she forced through her throat.

'Mom will die. They will kill her.'

Something turned in the eyes watching her. The hand on her shoulder tightened momentarily.

'She won't. They won't.'

Mr. Carter's voice didn't change, but Livy suddenly believed him.

Believed him without any doubt. In the same way she knew that Margie, her bestie, would never leave her side.

He moved her to the side, gently, and bent down and to her surprise, a door opened where they were standing.

He reached down and a light came on.

She peered over his shoulder and saw steps. Wooden steps.

He went down halfway, reached out for her and carried her down the steps.

Her eyes grew round when she took in the small room.

It was yellow and orange. It was warm.

It had a couch, a TV, books, a water cooler.

It had a refrigerator.

Mr. Carter led her to the couch and arranged a blanket over her.

'I'll be back. Nothing will happen to you or your mom.'

Livy nodded her head.

She knew he would.

Just as she knew the sun would rise tomorrow.

Hunting You

Chapter 21

Chloe stood in front of the approaching SUV, the second one.

Petite, finely featured, Chloe could stop traffic at any time of the day, anywhere.

At night in Milton Mills, with just one vehicle on the street, halting traffic was child's play.

She squinted when the bright beams hit her, didn't respond when a voice yelled out at her.

The SUV came to a halt, its engine growling softly in the night, the only sound in the darkness.

Three heads bobbed inside before one emerged. 'You got a death wish, lady?'

Chloe didn't reply.

The voice came back, irritation growing in it. 'Get the hell outta our way, babe.'

Chloe shifted weight on her feet, brushed her hair back.

A muttered curse came from inside. Something that sounded like *bitch.*

The passenger door opened and a gangbanger emerged. Tall, dark, tattooed, he looked around, walked cautiously toward Chloe.

'You don't speak English, lady? You gotta clear out.'

His hot breath stank of garlic and sweat. His left hand had a gun, his right was empty.

The right hand came up, with it came a leer on his face. 'You offering, honey?'

The hand reached out to touch her face.

She exploded into action.

She trapped his hand, slid a hip between his legs, pivoted and hurled the man across concrete. The barrel of her Glock came down between the thug's eyes before he could recover, and rendered him unconscious.

Simultaneously, two shadows raced from the sides of the road, smashed the windows, pointed guns at the two hoods inside.

It was swift, brutal, smooth.

'Where's our friend?' Roger asked when they had finished securing the men.

Broker glanced at the screen on his phone.

'Doing Zeb stuff.'

'Cezar is dead.'

Jenny Wade's voice was hoarse from screaming. She licked her dry lips, her eyes following the man who paced in front of her.

Boiler.

Her lips were split, her nose felt like it was broken, her right thigh twitched and trembled involuntarily.

She refused to look down at her leg. She had thrown up till her body was empty, but looking at the gash in her thigh would set her off on wracking, dry heaves.

Gash. Her mind shied away from using a stronger word.

Cezar had described Boiler at length to her. She had recognized him the moment he had entered her home. She had known in that terrifying instant that she wouldn't live out the night.

She had screamed at Livy to run, had dodged around the dining table to escape herself, but Boiler caught her easily.

He slapped her once, a flat-handed blow that caught her flush on her face and broke her nose.

She fell, crawled further away, rage filling her, drowning out the fear. She shouted again, at Livy to escape, grabbed a wooden chair and hurled it at Boiler, a lioness protecting her brood.

Boiler didn't duck, didn't even flinch.

The chair caught him on the shoulder, a leg broke, but Boiler stood implacable.

He came after her, she darted round the table.

One of his goons caught her, pushed her back into Boiler's reach.

He slapped her.

'Where's Cezar?' he asked as if discussing the weather.

He didn't give her time to respond. The bat-like hand caught her and brought her down.

The side of the table gouged into her thigh and drew blood.

She gasped and bit her lips hard to stifle a cry. Her vision dimmed for a second and when it cleared, she tried to rise.

Rough hands grabbed her, hauled her, and dumped her in the chair. Boiler's men, one of them Knuckles, whom she had seen a couple of times, tied her and stepped back.

Boiler came forward.

She heard the sound on the stairs, saw her daughter's scared face and with all the remaining breath in her, shouted at Livy to run.

Livy disappeared.

Boiler nodded lazily at two men who hustled up the stairs and tried to break down the locked door.

Jenny took advantage of the distraction and head butted Boiler.

It would have been effective if she had been free. It might have worked if she had been standing.

Her head lost most of its power and landed almost softly in his midriff.

He flung her back and crouched in front of her.

'Where's Cezar?'

'He's dead,' she spat at him.

He blinked once.

His hand moved faster than her eyes could comprehend. Something flashed.

Seconds later, white fire lanced through her when his knife buried deep in her thigh, where the table had bit.

She screamed and sobbed.

No one came to her help.

She looked once at the blade stuck in her leg and threw up. Again and again, till her body trembled and shivered.

Knuckles came forward and hurled a bucket of water on her. The cold shocked her and sucked her breath away.

She didn't feel the knife drawing out till Boiler sat and waved it in front of her.

'Cezar is dead.'

He grabbed her hair and raised her head.

'How?'

'Stroke. He had two, when he was with you. The third one killed him.' She spat in his face.

'Stroke? He was young, fit. Maybe you overworked him.'

She saw red at Knuckles snigger, leaned forward and smashed her forehead against Boiler's nose.

Cezar had taught her a few tricks.

Boiler reared back, lost his balance, recovered, and rose.

The two men entered, before he could retaliate.

Boiler raised an eyebrow.

'We didn't find her.'

'Did you check the neighbors?'

'There's only one. Carter. Ajdan is in that house.'

'Go search the streets.'

Livy had escaped!

Jenny looked down to hide the triumphant look in her eyes, the surge of adrenaline. Her baby was out there, alive.

If she could survive the night ...

The cold blade pricked her neck, drawing her eyes back to Boiler.

'We'll find her. She won't get far.'

Boiler's eyes shone with a green light. 'Then, my men will play with her.'

The scream that escaped Jenny's throat turned into a shriek when the knife entered her left shoulder and twisted.

'Let's start again.'

Boiler questioned her. Before and after each response, he cut her. Light cuts that bled, that gave the appearance of deeper injuries.

She fainted a couple of times. Knuckles revived her with water.

She stuck to her story.

That she and Cezar had drifted from city to city soon after going into witness protection. They hadn't stuck to the jobs they had been given, preferring to enjoy their freedom.

San Francisco, Los Angeles, Philly, Miami, Chicago, they spent a few weeks or months in each city, taking odd jobs.

She didn't know who Parker was.

He pricked her. She fainted.

When she came to, she still didn't know who Parker was.

'Where did he die?'

She didn't respond. Her head fell forward, her hair covering her face.

He jerked her face up and slapped her.

'Where did he die?'

'Connecticut.' Her voice was dull.

She was slipping away. He had to dial up his act.

'Where's the money?'

She mumbled something.

He pricked her.

She jerked as if stung.

'Where's the money?'

'It's gone.'

He thought he misheard her.

'Gone?'

She nodded.

'Gone where?'

He brought the knife down on her other thigh.

Her shriek tore through the air and rang through the silent house.

Zeb came across the two men searching in the open park in front of Jenny Wade's house.

They were moving slowly, searching behind trees and underneath benches.

Their guns were out, they covered one another, but they were casual. The town was theirs; there was no need to be razor sharp.

How long would the girl stay hidden?

He came behind the first man who was lagging behind his partner.

Zeb's shoes didn't make a sound; they distributed his weight evenly, lightly.

One moment he was creeping behind the thug, the next the gangbanger was falling, a single blow felling him.

His partner turned, his gun arm rising, his mouth opened to yell.

The warning didn't emerge.

Zeb grabbed his throat with one hand, disarmed him with ease, and squeezed.

'How many men inside?'

The man grunted and gasped.

A scream sounded from inside.

Zeb heard it. The hood heard it. There wasn't any other neighbor to hear it.

'How many?'

The hood told him.

'Where's the money?'

The voice came from far away, through the darkness surrounding Jenny Wade.

She wanted to embrace its warmth, but something held her back.

She squirreled away at what was holding her back.

It was Livy.

She would not die as long as her daughter was out there.

Livy's face blurred in front of her, became clear. Her giggle swept through her.

Jenny Wade decided not to die.

She had convinced Cezar to quit the gang. She had made him give up the money.

She had Livy.

She hadn't come this far to curl up and die.

'Where's the money?' This time the voice was sharper.

Everything came back to her, the room, Knuckles, another hood, and Boiler.

She laughed despite her condition.

It didn't come out as a laugh, but Boiler recognized the sound.

'Gave it away.'

'What? What did you say?'

'Gave it away. To charities.'

She laughed again.

The knife swung toward her thigh.

The door opened behind Knuckles.

A man stepped in the room and faced her.

She frowned.

She recognized him. Where had she seen him before?

The knife punctured her jeans and its point pricked her skin.

The pain cleared her fog.

Mr. Carter! What was he doing here?

She must have mumbled something because the knife left her.

The room felt as if it was underwater.

She saw Mr. Carter grow. No, that didn't make sense. He was already a grown man.

She squinted her eyes.

He was not growing.

His arm was rising. Something was at the end of it.

The report was curiously mild.

The man next to Knuckles fell.

Knuckles was diving, reaching for his gun. It was rising.

Another report sounded. Then another and a third.

Knuckles fell back as if punched back by a giant fist. His head became a watermelon.

No, it didn't.

It became what a melon became when squashed.

A fourth report sounded.

Boiler moved.

Boiler knew something was wrong the moment Wade mumbled something that suspiciously sounded like Carter.

He leaned closer to hear and found her attention was behind him.

Something's wrong.

He whirled round, spotted the figure at the door.

The figure moved, one of his men went down. More shots sounded, so close, they felt like one trigger burst.

Boiler moved.

He leapt, darted behind Wade's chair, used her as cover, searched for the gun in his waist.

Knuckles was down. The other hood was down.

His gun rose.

Carter was moving toward him.

Carter's gun was steady, trained on him.

Boiler was behind Wade.

He fired.

Carter staggered, lost his gun.

Boiler's lips curled in triumph.

He started to depress the trigger again.

Then Cezar's bitch had to play a hand.

She hurled herself to the side, fell along with the chair.

Now Boiler was exposed.

Carter was still coming.

Fast. Low. Deadly.

Kevlar!

Boiler couldn't complete the thought. Carter smashed into him, yanked his gun hand upward and smashed it against the wall.

The gun fell.

His shoulder crushed Boiler's ribs, squeezed his breath away.

Boiler grunted, reared his head back, and struck Carter's face like a pile driver.

He felt a shiver go through Carter, but his hold didn't loosen.

Instead he did something Boiler didn't anticipate.

His hand curled around Boiler's head, crushed it against his face, like a lover's embrace.

The fist that sank into Boiler wasn't like any lover's.

It spread hot agony in him, exploding in his body, making him groan loudly. He thought something cracked.

A rib.

Boiler had fought in Ukraine. He ruled Miami. Carter wasn't going to get the best of him.

He summoned his strength, snapped his hands up and managed to break Carter's hold.

Howling like a wolf, he followed through, flinging Carter against the far wall as if he was a ragdoll.

He followed, halted.

Carter didn't bounce and fall off the wall.

He bounced against it with his feet, landed like a cat, grabbed a chair and hurled it at Boiler.

Boiler didn't duck fast enough.

A leg caught him in the cheek. His face split open.

Carter was on him, snapping his head with a quick jab, punching the broken rib, spearing fire in him.

Boiler shaped his fury into a hammer, let it loose against Carter.

The hammer sailed over Carter's shoulder, was gripped, and then it was Boiler who was flying and crashing against the wall.

He roared, left the floor in a dive, met Carter's knee with his face.

His nose broke. He thought his jaw broke. He fell back. He embraced the pain, bathed in it, used it to fuel his rage.

He landed on the floor.

Next to the knife he had used on Wade.

He grabbed it. Pulled Jenny Wade by her hair, dragged her along with the chair, pulled her up.

His knife arced down. Wade screamed.

His hand met resistance, halted.

Carter's hand gripped his wrist and arrested its downward slide.

The two men strained, throwing their weight behind their limbs, sweat pouring down their faces, blood soaking Boiler's shirt.

Boiler's lips drew back. He knew he had the upper hand.

Carter wouldn't try anything else or his arresting grip would weaken and the knife would sink into Cezar's woman.

'She'll die. In front of you.'

Something seemed to change in Carter.

188

The brown eyes changed, became flat, hard. Walls.

The hand that was trembling with the effort of holding his knife hand back, stopped trembling.

It became solid. Like a block of concrete.

Boiler felt Carter's body behind the block, all hardness and forward motion.

Carter moved. The knife dipped.

Towards Boiler.

Boiler strained, sucked in great gulps of air, but couldn't break Carter's lock.

He dropped Wade, swung a punch at Carter.

It landed on his temple. He didn't blink.

He brought a leg up, kicked out at Carter.

Carter's left hand folded, his elbow pointed like an arrow and met Boiler's kick.

Blackness raced through Boiler.

He heard himself groaning.

He ditched the attack, clasped both hands on the knife, gritted his teeth, and attempted to dislodge Carter.

Time seemed to stand still. Noise seemed to recede, other than their breathing, and struggling on the floor.

The door slammed open. Shadows rushed in.

He didn't turn. It would be his men. If they weren't, his men would take care of whoever the intruders were. He had enough feet on the ground.

Carter didn't turn either.

Someone shouted. Someone else responded.

Light flashed. A report sounded. More reports sounded.

The blade didn't waver. It was still pointing to his left and down, where Wade had been.

She was now lying on the floor, her eyes watching them in sick fascination.

More reports sounded, like a roll of thunder.

Carter let go silently.

The blade leapt in the air, moved to the left.

Boiler reacted, his synapses moved to correct its flight, turn its killing arc.

Carter kicked Wade's chair. It scraped away, dragging her with it

The blade's flight turned, Boiler lunged.

His eyes widened in sudden shock when his wrist became putty, the knife seemed to twist in his grip.

Carter spoke for the first time.
'Never again.'
The knife disappeared.
Inside Boiler.

Chapter 22

Jenny was sleeping on a warm, soft bed. She was floating blissfully, images and memories drifting in her mind.

Happy times with Cezar. Laughter, playing in their backyard. She smiled in her sleep. If this was Heaven, she didn't want to wake.

More memories came. Livy and her at the dining table, her daughter's excited narration of the day. She, marking her school work. The men entering her dining room. Boiler.

Jenny stirred uneasily. The orange and warmth faded. A memory came, of Boiler's green eyes piercing hers, something glinting in his hand. He too faded. All she could remember was sound and shouting.

Another face, initially blurred. It sharpened into Mr. Carter's.

He spoke. She strained to hear him.

'You'll be fine.'

Jenny smiled. This was a first. Mr. Carter hadn't ever spoken to her till then.

His lips moved again.

'Olivia is safe.'

Livy? Why wouldn't she be safe?

Livy.

It all came back to her in a rush.

Her eyes flew open.

She was in her room, in her bed, snuggled under her favorite comforter. Her thighs throbbed, her shoulder burned dully. She pushed the blanket down and surveyed herself.

She was dressed in an old T-shirt and sweatpants, underneath which she was bandaged in places. On her thighs and shoulders; all those places where Boiler had cut her.

She flexed her toes and fingers. They moved.

She listened. There was a faint murmur of voices from outside, but her house felt warm and safe.

Like a home.

Livy burst in the room, a whirlwind of energy and blonde curls.

She took one look at her mother and yelled to the people outside.

'Mom's awake!'

Pike bustled in followed by Chuck and Bundy and the three waited patiently while mother and daughter exchanged hugs, kisses, and smiles and shed a few tears.

Pike beamed at her when Livy skipped out of the room. 'How're you feeling?'

'Like I've been poked with a sharp knife. Several times.' She laughed.

'Who bandaged and dressed me?'

'Mr. Carter. He's a man of many talents.'

'Good man. Didn't speak a word.' Chuck said gruffly. Anyone who didn't waste breath was a go-to guy in his books.

Bundy read Jenny's wandering gaze around her room. 'You didn't want to be taken to the hospital. You were very insistent about that. No cops. No hospital.'

He held his right wrist up and brandished the discoloration around it. 'You grabbed me tighter than a vice and didn't let go until we promised.'

'Mr. Carter – he had some experience of such wounds, he said – had a look at yours and said they looked worse than they really were. Boiler was going more for effect, initially, than real harm. It was the shock that made you lose consciousness, not the loss of blood or serious damage. You'll have a limp for a while, but that will go away soon.'

He swallowed. 'However, if Mr. Carter hadn't come in time, that knife dude would have gotten down to serious business.'

Jenny shivered and drew the comforter tighter. 'Where is Mr. Carter?'

Two people swept in the room before any of them could answer.

A woman in the lead, a man behind her. Both of them in suits and brought with them a formal manner.

'Jenny, I'm FBI Special Agent in Charge, Sarah Burke and this is Special Agent Mark Kowalski.'

They flashed badges at her. 'I lead a task force that investigates gang crimes, high profile crimes... anything that doesn't get solved or no one else wants to touch, comes to me.' She smiled deprecatingly.

'You have had an eventful night. Are you up to answering a few questions?'

Jenny nodded and began narrating, without waiting for the questions.

Behind the FBI agents she saw Pike nodded approvingly at

her recital, till Burke asked a question.

'Who killed Boiler and the others?'

Pike put his finger to his lips. She paused, trying to figure out what Pike wanted her to say.

What does he want to hide from the Feds?

Pike stepped in smoothly before she could reply. 'Like we said, ma'am, they were FBI agents. They didn't give names, were masked and were outfitted like your Hostage Rescue Teams. They shouted they were the FBI.'

'And if that wasn't clear enough, their jackets were stenciled with the same three letters,' Bundy added, drily.

'A bunch of them rescued us from the cellar.' Chuck broke his word count quota for the day. 'Didn't wait for our thanks. Made sure we were okay and then disappeared. They said they had other gang members to apprehend.'

'I was asking Jenny Wade.' Burke's voice was icy.

'I don't remember much,' Jenny answered truthfully.

'I was drifting off. I was in shock and thought I was dying. All I remember is the door bursting open, voices shouting. The men were masked and there were some letters on their vests, but I was too far gone to read them.'

She saw Pike nodded approvingly.

He stepped forward, irritation on his face and in his voice. 'With respect, ma'am, you should know all this. The lead agent, or whatever you folks call him, said you would be coming later to check on us.'

Jenny was good at reading people. She had to be.

Years of living with Cezar, of meeting some of his *friends,* the years when they lived in cities, always looking over their shoulder, had taught her to look beyond what people said.

She saw the FBI agents were confused but hid it well, behind their professional demeanor.

What's going on? Why's Pike hiding Mr. Carter's identity?

Burke regarded the three men for a long while, letting the silence build. They didn't break.

She turned to Jenny finally. 'Why were they after you, ma'am?'

Jenny saw the questioning looks in her friends' eyes and knew she owed them an explanation too.

'I was married to a guy called Cezar. He was a drug dealer in Virginia, initially in Miami, in a gang bossed by a scary man who was called Big G.'

'Cezar and Big G were close. They were initially in another inner city gang in Miami, but Big G was ambitious and he broke away to set up his own outfit. Big G was ruthless; he had men with him who were equally ruthless. Boiler was one of those men. In no time, the gang's criminal reach ran from the north to the south.'

She drank from the glass Chuck handed and looked at her friends.

Pike's eyes were shocked, as were Bundy and Chuck's. She hoped they would forgive her for her deceit.

She hadn't lied to any of them. She just had never told them who she was and where she came from. They had accepted her, had made her feel welcome, at home.

'Big G asked Cezar to run the Virginia operations for the gang. What Big G said, Cezar did. I moved with him, but by then, I was sick of this life. I wanted Cezar to quit.'

She glossed over the arguments, the fights, and the late night screaming matches.

'Cezar said Big G would kill both of us. It wouldn't be a pleasant death.' She shivered. 'I got a taste of it last night. If,' she caught herself in time, 'your agents hadn't come in time; I would be slashed to death. Slowly. That was Boiler's specialty.'

'Big G got captured in Mexico, Boiler took over the gang. We heard that Big G still ran the gang from inside. Nothing changed.'

'There was a way out, however.'

She told about the initial meetings with the FBI, with the Special Agent in Charge of the Richmond office. She gave them names.

Kowalski pulled out a tablet and started punching keys.

Checking up on my story.

She walked them through the details, the excitement and fear of escaping the life they had, starting a new one. Of their meetings with the Marshals, their sifting through several identities, selecting the one she had now. A school teacher.

'We would be based in a small town in Connecticut.' She mentioned the name. 'We would be free.'

'We lived in that town for a while, but both of us had always wanted to see the rest of the country. We traveled. All over the country, despite the warning from the Marshals. We lived in a state of fear, always looking out, looking for strangers, gangbangers. But we enjoyed the freedom.'

She sighed. 'What I didn't know was that Cezar had Big G's money. He stole thirty million dollars from the gang.'

Someone gasped. She nodded. It was a heck of a lot of money.

'Cezar had been stealing for a long time, and that built up.'

She saw the light dawning in the FBI agents, in her friends, when they made the connection. 'That's right. Boiler was after the money.'

'Things changed the moment I knew this. We couldn't keep traveling the way we did, someone would spot us. The gang had a reach across the country, either through its own presence or through other gangs.'

'We couldn't return the money. Boiler would kill us.'

She smiled, a joyous, carefree smile. 'We gave the money to charities. That's a lot of money, but there are thousands of charities in the country. Each one got at least fifty thousand dollars. Some got twice that.'

She saw the skepticism in the Feds. 'Pike, there's a safe in that wardrobe over there.'

She gave him the combination. There would be no more secrets from her friends.

'In a plastic file folder right at the bottom, there will be a list.'

Pike searched, found the folder, opened it, and rifled through the various papers till he came to the list.

The list ran to three sheets and had names, addresses, amounts, and dates on it.

'You can cross check those deposits with the charities. You can make copies.'

Kowalski disappeared. Chuck accompanied him.

'Where's Cezar?' Burke asked when they returned.

Jenny sensed she was struggling with taking it all in, but she didn't show. Her voice was cool; her face didn't show any emotion.

'Cezar died, just after Livy's birth. The stress had been getting to him. He had a couple of strokes while in the gang. The third killed him. I buried him in Connecticut.'

She mentioned the church, the graveyard.

'I came to this village five years back. It fit the profile of the town the Marshals had initially placed us in. I restarted the life they had built for me, only in a different town.'

She stopped, tired but relieved that it was all out in the open now. No more hiding, no more looking behind her shoulder. No more secrets from her friends.

Pike handed her another glass of water. She emptied it and flopped back on her bed.

'What now?' She asked the agents.

Burke and Kowalski exchanged a glance. 'That's quite a story, ma'am. We'll have to check it out thoroughly, but I'm sure it'll stack up.'

'We have a few more questions. They won't take long.' She turned to Pike. 'Why didn't you take her to a hospital, or call 911?'

'She didn't want us to. She was very vocal about it. Why would we call 911 when your agents were here?' Pike smirked.

'Who dressed her wounds?' Burke's posture said she knew the answer.

'One of your agents. Like I said, they didn't give out names, ma'am. They didn't hand out business cards. The only name they mentioned was yours. They gave me your number, said you would be coming. I didn't wait, and called you.' Pike had a hard time controlling a grin.

Burke's voice turned hard. 'Mr. Pike, you don't seem to be taking this seriously. May I warn you that you could get into all sorts of trouble for misleading the FBI.'

Pike's face was innocent. 'Any more trouble than winding up dead at the hands of gangsters, ma'am?'

Burke's body wilted for a nanosecond before recovering. 'Where are the bodies?'

Pike gave astonished. His voice became wondering. 'Why, ma'am, your men took them.'

Burke cursed for a good ten minutes, words and phrases spilling out that she had never used in her career.

She whirled on Kowalski when she had finished. 'If it ever gets out that I swore, I'll –.'

Kowalski put up a palm in peace. 'I get it. I'll end up polishing shoes somewhere or washing dishes in some roadside diner.'

'You'll end up polishing shoes for those who are washing dishes,' Burke warned him.

'Of course.'

They stared out from the inside of their SUV, looking over

the village at a scene that was straight out of a picture postcard.

Pristine white church. Lush green lawns. Happy smiling people.

'What do you make of it?' Kowalski asked.

'If I knew, I wouldn't be sitting here, listening to your moronic questions,' she growled in frustration.

'How did we ever get to this?' She untied her ponytail, retied it, but even that gesture didn't calm her.

Of course she knew how they had gotten here.

The call had come at four a.m. that morning, rousing her from a deep sleep. Saturdays were her days off. She didn't go on her ten-mile run on those days, preferring to burrow under her blankets and sleep late.

Saturdays were when Special Agent in Charge Sarah Burke disappeared and girl-next-door, Sarah, appeared.

Not this Saturday.

The phone roused her and when she answered, a male voice came on.

'Special Agent in Charge, Sarah Burke?'

'Yeah, how did you get this number?' She groped for the night lamp, turned it on and peered at the number on the screen.

There wasn't one.

'Your agent gave it to me, ma'am. My name is Pike. I'm calling you from Milton Mills, New Hampshire.'

The voice warmed. 'Your men did a splendid job, ma'am. They saved our village from these thugs. Saved our lives. I know it's early, and they said you were coming, but I just had to call you and thank you.'

My men? Saved a village? Coming? What? Where? How?

'Can you run through that again, Mr. Pike? I'm behind with my reports.'

Nice one, Burke.

'Not at all, ma'am,' Pike replied.

Was that a smug tone?

She grabbed her other phone, typed out a hasty text to Kowalski. She didn't care if that woke him up.

Do you know anything about a takedown in Milton Mills?

'You there, ma'am?'

'Yeah, go on.' Gone was her sleep. She turned on the TV, muted it and flipped through various news channels.

Nothing on Milton Mills.

Pike explained at length.

'And you say these men identified themselves as FBI agents?'

'That's right, ma'am.'

'How many of them were there?'

'Dunno man. I saw five, but there could be more. They came, they saw, they conquered.'

He chuckled at his own joke.

'What did the gang want?'

'No clue, ma'am. They locked us up and were torturing a woman, a resident, when thankfully, your men burst in.'

His voice turned curious. 'Your men didn't report to you, ma'am?'

'I'm sure they did. Like I said, I'm behind. I'm juggling several cases.'

Nice save, Burke.

Pike wound down. 'Thank you again, ma'am. You folks saved our bacon today. I hope you find who these folks were and why they were camped in our village. I'll be writing to your Director, thanking him for the fine job you did.'

No!

'Mr. Pike, our investigations are still ongoing. I will appreciate if you held back from contacting the Director, for the time being.'

Lame, Burke.

He bought it.

'Sure, I'll back off, ma'am. Well, I gotta go. Thank you again, ma'am. You folks do the nation proud. I'll see you in the village.'

'Wait! Did my agent mention his name?'

'No, ma'am. None of them gave any names.'

It took an hour to rouse her crew and brief them. Not one had a clue.

She ordered them to rendezvous at Reagan in forty-five minutes, got Kowalski to arrange vehicles for them at Portsmouth International Airport in Pease.

She brushed, showered, dressed, packed her gear, her mind whirling all the while, but she was no closer to finding answers.

Till now.

And she still didn't have answers.

Kowalski and she watched a woman push a baby carriage, glance curiously at the SUV and move on.

They had interviewed the captives from the bar. All of them told the same story that Pike had.

The solitary man in the bar had hit on Burke. Had suggested a celebratory drink.

To thank her for rescuing them, was how he had put it.

Kowalski had a hard time concealing his mirth.

No other residents had any more insight.

The house next to Wade's was empty. No one knew where the owner was.

'Did you find out who occupies the next door house?'

Kowalski cursed, bent to his tablet.

Pike peered from Jenny's window, spotted the Feds' SUV parked a few homes away, and came back feeling satisfied.

'What's going on Pike?' Jenny demanded in a loud whisper.

Livy was on the bed. Sleeping, with teddy, smiling now that her universe was back to where it had been. She had told Jenny about her adventure.

That was what she called it. She said that secret place Mr. Carter had, was cool. It was so comfortable that she had slept. The next thing she knew, she was back in her home, next to Mom.

Jenny asked her where the secret hide was. Livy pursed her lips. It was a secret. She had pinkie-sworn to Mr. Carter.

Jenny didn't push it. Livy would tell her in good time. Her daughter couldn't keep secrets.

She, Pike, Chuck, and Bundy had talked at length. She had cried, gut wrenching sobs that seemed to wash away the past and had left her calmer. She apologized for keeping her past from them.

Chuck surprised them. The taciturn bartender hugged her and patted her back.

'The past don't matter, girl. The present and the future do.'

That ended *that* discussion, but Jenny had to ask.

'Why did you lie to them, Pike? They're FBI agents for chrissakes! Why didn't you tell them about Mr. Carter?'

'He asked us not to,' Pike answered simply.

Pike and the others had trotted behind the black man and the blond guy, following them to Jenny Wade's house.

He saw the SUVs in front of her house, his fears mounted. He asked a question, but got a jerked head in return.

He, Chuck, and Bundy rushed inside and stopped.

Bodies all over. That was the first thought that came to his mind.

Two by the door. Another against the wall.

A fourth, nearby.

No not a body. That was Jenny. Someone was tending to her.

He hurried across and gasped.

That someone was Mr. Carter.

He looked up once but didn't speak to Pike.

Pike saw his hands were surprisingly gentle as they moved over Jenny's body, assessing her injuries.

'She's in shock. None of these are serious cuts. He was toying with her,' he murmured to no one.

'Chloe?'

'Here.' Pike moved back dumbly to let a petite woman pass.

She crouched next to Mr. Carter, handed him a medical kit and helped him dress Jenny's wounds.

Mr. Carter carried her upstairs to her room, disappeared for several moments while Pike and the other residents aimlessly milled around and watched the strangers drag the dead away.

Mr. Carter returned. He had Olivia in his arms.

'She's sleeping,' he answered Pike's unspoken question.

Pike looked at him and the four other men and three women, when he returned downstairs.

All eight were outfitted in vests, combat suits, the kind he saw on several TV shows. The men had a hard edge to them that was apparent despite their casual stance. The women looked equally competent.

Two of them are twins.

'Shall I call 911?' he asked diffidently.

Pike was a take-charge man, but here, he had relinquished control to Mr. Carter. To his surprise, he found he was okay with that.

He didn't know what was going on. But he suspected his fellow resident knew and also knew what had to be done.

He wasn't surprised when Mr. Carter shook his head. 'No need.'

'We gotta explain all this.'

Mr. Carter handed him a phone. 'There's a number on that. The first number on the dialed list. It's the number for FBI Special Agent in Charge, Sarah Burke. Call her.'

Pike felt himself smiling foolishly when he heard the story Mr. Carter spun out. This would keep his buddies entertained for years.

He asked one question before he started dialing. 'Are you good guys?'

The black man chuckled. 'What do you think, sir?'

Sir.

Pike observed him carefully. Looked at the rest of the strangers and lastly at Mr. Carter.

Heck, if these were the bad guys, they were going to Hell in any case.

He called the FBI agent.

Jenny heard in silence, her hand absently stroking her daughter's curls.

'He didn't tell you anything?'

'Nope. He and his crew loaded the bodies in their vehicles and they just took off.'

'Where?'

'Heck if I know.'

Kowalski chuckled, rousing Burke from deep thought. The chuckle turned into laughter.

Deep gusts that arose from his center.

Burke stared at him as if he had lost his mind.

Maybe he had. This case was driving all of them nuts.

'You know who owns that house?' Kowalski wheezed.

'No I don't. That's why I asked you to check,' Burke replied curtly.

Kowalski calmed down, wiped his face with a tissue and looked at her with a smile.

'You're gonna love this.'

'You know that owner. You've met him a few times.'

'Who is it?' Burke asked through gritted teeth. She didn't like playing games.

'Zeb Carter.'

Burke fell back as if punched, her eyes widening, looking past Kowalski, down the street, where Wade's house was visible and just past it, the neighboring house.

She sat there as synapses fired, neurons floated and buzzed and somehow connections were made in a way that billions of years of evolution had perfected.

Who else? she thought dimly, over the cacophony of pieces slotting into place.

Who else has the connections, the ability?   Who else wouldn't want credit?

'Where is he?'

No one came close to Big G.

He heard the news Saturday evening. A whisper that was passed to him in the shower stalls from another inmate who was visited by family earlier in the day.

Boiler was dead. Killed by the FBI.

The Feds were cracking down on his gang.

Big G went on a tear. He smashed the inmate's head against the concrete wall. He punched another inmate and broke a third one's leg.

The guards came rushing in.

He groined one, poked another's eye before they clubbed him, subdued him, chained him, and hauled him back to solitary.

Today was Sunday.

His killing mood hadn't dissipated, but he had no one to vent on.

Gang gone. Money gone. Karel gone.

Big G alone lived.

He made a vow. He would come out of this alive.

He would rebuild his gang.

He would go after those agents who murdered Karel. He would go after that bitch and recover his money.

He rattled his cage and shouted loudly.

He needed a shower.

The guards came. Four of them.

Two of them trained shotguns at him, while the two others fell in behind.

The solitary cells were separated from the showers by a sliding, barred gate.

Cameras were all over and when Big G approached the gate, it swung back silently and shut behind him.

He was all alone in the showers.

He turned on the tap, let the water flow on him.

The guards watched him impassively through the bars.

He would kill them too.

Big G turned his back on them, reached out for the thin

sliver that passed for soap, and lathered himself.

The lights went out.

Big G turned and saw it was just the showers that were dark. The cells were brightly lit; the guards were still watching him.

'Hey,' he called out. 'I can't see. Turn on the damned lights.'

They didn't respond.

'Can you hear me?' he shouted, his rage bubbling over.

Big G deserved a response.

'They won't respond.'

The voice came from behind. Indifferent. Bored.

Big G whirled around. There were ten showers, a changing room, nothing else.

He thought he saw a shadow in the far end.

'Who are you?' he asked suspiciously.

He moved back to the shower stall. Reached behind with his hands. Bent as if searching for the bar of soap and searched for the shiv that he had concealed in a crack in the floor.

The shadow didn't answer.

Big G rose.

'Hey,' he called out to the guards. 'There's some dude here.'

The guards turned their backs on him. Started walking away.

What the fuck?

'They won't interfere.'

'Interfere with what?' he shouted, anger lacing his voice, but also fear.

Anyone who could turn lights off, get the guards to ignore him, was *someone*.

The shadow didn't answer.

'Who are you?' Big G shouted again. That was his default tone now. It was what he used to intimidate, to make others cower.

It was also his tone when he went into combat mode.

The shadow moved. 'I'm the one who killed Boiler.'

Big G thrust with the shiv, a cutting motion that had disemboweled several victims.

He disemboweled empty air.

The shadow was no longer there.

Trap.

Big G turned swiftly but not fast enough to evade the block of concrete that hit him.

The blow to his midriff staggered him.

Darkness swam in his vision.

He shook his head to clear it away.

He was Big G. He ran one of the largest gangs in the country. He ran this prison.

The shadow moved again.

This time Big G crouched as low as he could, jabbed fast and straight.

Something clasped his wrist, a grip so painful that he cried in agony. He went flying, crashed against the wall, and slid to the floor.

He thrust himself upward as quickly as he could.

He would fight. He would escape. He would kill –.

Something, a knee, smashed his face. He reached out blindly, his hands were swatted away.

His groans and shouts went unanswered. No guards came rushing in.

His attacker moved silently. All Big G could see, through one good eye, was a shadow.

The shadow became smaller and before he knew what was happening, he was lifted. Easily.

Now Big G could see the assailant's eyes. They were brown. Or maybe black.

Their color didn't matter anymore because the assailant hurled him against the wall. Some kind of martial arts throw.

Big G bounced off concrete.

He didn't hear the attacker approach.

He didn't feel the chokehold that was applied.

Big G was beyond hearing. Beyond caring.

Beyond living.

One month from the events in Milton Mills, Olivia spotted Zeb.

He was doing that thing with his hands and legs. She had to go to school or else she would have copied his actions.

She dressed in a mad rush, ran down the stairs, and announced to her mom that their neighbor was back.

She waited impatiently for the school bus, to break the news to Margie.

Her mom watched her daughter board the bus, looked out once at her neighbor's house, but as usual didn't spot him.

Big G's death hadn't made front page news, but it reached

her because she had set an alert for his name.

She had cried that night, in the aloneness of her bathroom. She had looked heavenward and thanked HIM. She had cried for lost years, had lain in the bathtub till her skin wrinkled, till the sobs turned into hiccups and died away.

She knew for certain her neighbor had something to do with Big G's death. She didn't require proof.

She knew a little of Mr. Carter by now.

Nothing had changed at Chuck's bar.

Zeb ordered his usual, exchanged nods with the silent bartender and went to his corner table.

He ate slowly, enjoying the rays of sunshine that came through a window and lit his table.

His friends were back in New York. All loose ends had been tied up.

The twins had wondered at his lack of surprise at their presence in the village.

'At the least, you could've pretended to be glad to see us, Zeb,' Beth had cried. Her warm hug belied the tone in her voice.

'Broker's not the only one who can keep tabs via the satellites,' he had countered.

The mystery behind Hank being mistaken for Cezar had been cleared up.

'It was some kind of virus,' Broker's baritone had been soft when he conveyed the news to Zeb. 'The Marshals aren't admitting it, but it swapped addresses from several Federal databases. Hank's details came from one of those. By a freakish coincidence, he and his wife, looked similar to Cezar and Jenny.'

Zeb didn't say anything. Nothing was there to be said. Luck played a role sometimes.

Luck had brought Hank into his life. He looked up, at the blue sky. Its hue reminded him of a pair of eyes.

Say hi to my wife and son, Hank.

The shout on TV brought him back. A ball game. No one was watching it.

The bar wasn't busy. A couple of families. A man in a suit tapping away on a laptop. At one of the tables, two men he recognized. Pike and Bundy.

Chuck went over to them, whispered something and they glanced in his direction.

Pike raised a glass in a silent toast. Zeb nodded in acknowledgement.

None of them came over and shook his hand or slapped his back or shared his space.

They weren't like that.

He rose when he had finished, dropped a few bills and left.

Chuck stopped him before he reached the door.

'That isn't required.' He thrust the bills back at Zeb.

Zeb made to protest, but a shout from across the room cut him off.

'Danged right. And if you stop coming here, he'll deliver food to your house and he'll keep doing it till it stacks up, blocks your door, and it floods into the street.'

Pike. Red-faced, but smiling broadly.

Zeb took back the bills, pocketed them and did something Milton Mills had never seen before.

He smiled.

Coming soon

Zero

Warriors Series, Book 8

BY Ty Patterson

Chapter 1

Washington D.C. is the center of the political universe. There are other cities that suck in more traffic and business; New York or London for example. There are other countries that wield as much economic clout as the United States. If China sneezes, the world's stock markets catch a cold.

However, when it comes to global political influence, the United States is still the foremost world power and its capital is at the heart of that.

Due to that white residence which is recognized the world over; it is also one of the most secure cities on the planet.

It is not just that residence that calls the city, home. There are various defense, intelligence, and investigative agencies that are headquartered in the city. Many of those agencies carry three-letter acronyms. Some of those agencies are unknown to the taxpayer and are hidden under layers of deception.

Not far from the city is that five-sided building; the largest office block in the world. It's an office of course, but it's also much more than that.

Washington D.C. is small compared to other world cities. It is less than sixty-four square miles and has a population of less than seven hundred thousand.

In comparison, New York is just under three hundred and five square miles, with over eight million people. London is well over six hundred and seven square miles and has a similar population to New York.

Despite such a concentration of agencies and political power, security in the Washington D.C. isn't obvious.

Gun toting police officers don't hang about on street corners. Cruisers patrol the streets of course, but if they are bristling with men and guns, it isn't apparent.

But the security apparatus is there, hidden, tucked away

and part of it springs to life when that motorcade emerges.

Then choppers and numerous patrol cars and motorcycle outriders appear and shut down streets and suddenly you can see uniforms and weapons and hard stares and dark shades all over.

The city resumes its somnolent state when the cavalcade disappears.

The Presidential View Hotel caters to tourists and businessmen and that animal species that's all too common in the city – lobbyists.

It's a small, intimate hotel, just over hundred rooms, a Michelin-starred restaurant adjacent to the lobby. The restaurant is well known in the city and always needs reservations.

The reason for the hotel's name is apparent if you step outside and face it and turn right. You'll see that white residence, the American flag flying proudly on top.

The more famous Jefferson Hotel is just a stone's throw away, diagonally opposite, on Sixteenth Street.

The president frequents the Jefferson occasionally. It is said there are tunnels that connect the Jefferson with that famous residence. Obviously, no one is going to confirm their existence.

Washington D.C. hasn't been attacked by terrorists in a while.

A while is a long time back though.

They came to the Presidential View in twos and threes. Most of them were clean shaven, the few who had facial hair, were neatly trimmed. One of the facial hair wearers, sported a moustache. A brown one. Another had a French beard and glasses.

They wore jeans or tracksuits and dark windbreakers. Some wore ball caps.

They all carried gym bags. They were heavy, but all fifteen of them carried the bags with ease.

Two of them came into the restaurant, lugging their bags, hung around as if waiting to be seated.

They drifted away when it looked like it would be a long wait. Both of them casually eyed the seated patrons, about thirty of them.

Neither of them saw the group of nine in the far corner.

Zeb saw them. He saw their bags. He saw their eyes run past his group. He read their body language. They hadn't come to be seated. They had come to see how the restaurant looked or felt.

Tourists. He half expected them to click pictures, but they didn't.

He turned his attention to his eight companions, who, along with the ninth, formed the Agency.

The Agency didn't have a three-letter acronym. Few people knew that it existed. Of those, only a handful knew of its true purpose. Those who knew, had security clearances that were off the scale.

The Agency took direct and proactive action against threats to the country. It went in where other deep black agencies hesitated.

Terrorists, organized crime, drug traffickers, armaments dealer, missing nuclear and chemical warheads – those and many others were the Agency's targets.

It had taken out bad guys in Syria, Iraq, Iran, Somalia, Indonesia, Pakistan, Afghanistan, France, Britain, Nigeria, and many more countries. It went where the threats were, regardless of national boundaries.

It had its own intel network that rivaled the best in the country; a network that Zeb and Broker had built.

Zebadiah Carter, Zeb, was its lead agent.

A seat away from him was Broker, the handsome, elderly one. An intelligence analyst who ran the logistics, the planning, and the intel for the Agency.

Broker was flanked by Bwana and Roger. Bwana was as tall as he was dark. He looked frightening. He was frightening when he was in combat mode. He was as gentle as kitten when he played civilian.

Roger could have modeled for the luxury couture brands. Instead he chose to be a Special Forces operative and that resulted in his joining Zeb.

Bear, as tall as Bwana, but with a thick beard, sat with Chloe, a petite brunette. They were a couple, in work and in life. They were the best close protection people Zeb had come across.

Meghan and Beth Peterson, twins, sat next to Chloe. Blonde, attractive, vivacious, and extremely intelligent. They supported Broker. They virtually ran the Agency and reduced

Broker to lounging around on a couch.

Most of them were ex Special Forces operatives, except Broker who had come from the Rangers, Chloe, who was from the 82nd Airborne, and the twins.

The twins were daughters of a celebrated cop in Jackson Hole. They had bumped into Zeb a while back and worn him down till he made them part of the crew.

At the head of the table sat Zeb's boss. Clare. She reported only to the president. She had never let the Commander-in-Chief down.

Zeb's crew was in town to celebrate Clare's birthday. She was in her late forties, the same age as Broker, but didn't look it. Her grey eyes were usually cool.

They were mirthful that day. All of them were. It was one of those rare periods of downtime for them.

Zeb turned to the entrance, smiling in response to a joke from Broker, and saw the two men departing.

He noticed their tracksuits first.

They didn't belong in the restaurant.

Tourists aren't known for their dress sense.

He then saw the gym bags. One of the men adjusted the bag on his shoulder; it tightened and for a moment straight lines and angles stood out in relief.

Must be some sporting team.

He laughed absentmindedly at something Meghan said.

Sports teams don't stay in this hotel. Which kind of game requires something straight or angled?

Ice hockey? Nothing going on now. Not in this part of the country. Field hockey? Not played here.

He ran the various sports in his mind, looking down at the table.

No game came to his mind.

When he raised his head, all of them had gone silent, were staring at him.

'What?' Meghan asked him.

He shook his head. He was overreacting.

'What?' She persisted.

He told them.

Broker rose. 'I'll have a look outside.'

He returned a few minutes later, looking relaxed from the outside, except for the pinched look in his eyes that only they recognized.

'Three men outside, all dressed similarly. Three gym bags. I collared a bellhop and asked him about the men. They aren't staying in the hotel.'

Mumbai.

The thought flashed in Zeb's mind.

In 2008 a bunch of terrorists had breezed through the city, shooting at will in a busy railway terminus and other public places.

In addition, they had shot through two high profile hotels. They had killed a hundred and sixty-four people before they themselves had been brought down.

Every security agency in the world had planned and prepared for Mumbai style attacks, since then.

It's Clare's birthday. Don't go looking for threats when none exist.

He forced himself to relax, reached out for his glass when the look on Broker's face stopped him.

'I accidentally brushed against one of the bags. It sounded metallic.'

'Where's he?' Zeb asked Clare urgently.

She knew what he was asking, pulled her phone out and made a brief call. Her shoulders relaxed. 'He isn't in town. No one is staying or visiting this hotel today.'

The warmth in her eyes disappeared. 'Let's deal with this. It could be nothing, but let's be sure.'

'If we approach them, they might just cut loose. The hotel's busy. Even the presence of cruisers might set them off.' Chloe, pragmatic, calm, collected.

'I don't think they're on a killing mission, or a suicidal mission. They would have opened up by now.' Bear added. 'This looks like a hostage deal.'

Zeb agreed and came to a decision. 'Broker, can Yuri hack into the hotel?'

Yuri was their friendly East European hacker, one of the best in that business. On another mission they had come across him and had offered him a deal.

Work for them, or take a bullet. Yuri took the former. He was loyal, never seemed to sleep and had jelled in very well with them.

Broker sniffed. 'I could, if I wasn't here. I'm sure he can too.' He made a discreet call, laughed once and ended it.

'He'll get onto it.'

'Ask him to penetrate the camera system. He should take it over only when I say so.'

Broker nodded, fired off a text.

Clare opened the menu which ran to several pages and flipped to the end. The hotel's layout and fire escape plans were marked in red on the last page. She studied it for a moment and turned it around to Zeb.

'How would you do it?'

Zeb had thought about it; the moment he had spotted the two men. 'I think they'll have around ten men. You don't need a lot to shut down a hotel. Once you control the entrance, the parking lot, the service entrances, you've taken it over.'

'This hotel has seven floors, fifteen rooms on each.' He had looked its details up before booking the table.

'This restaurant is the only dining room they have. There's a gym and swimming pool next to the basement parking lot.'

He paused, laid it out in his mind, continued. 'One man on the roof. Nothing there, one man will do. Two men on the uppermost floor – one in the corridor, one in the stairwell. Such pairing every few floors, right down to the ground floor.'

'Control the cameras, take over the phones, computers and security, shut down the entrances, and the hotel is captured.'

They sat in silence mulling it over. None of them objected. They had experienced hostage situations before, knew capturing such a hotel wasn't difficult.

'We should've brought in India style hotel checks,' Bwana commented darkly.

After the Mumbai attacks, every major hotel in that country had installed bag scanners. Every visitor to the hotel was frisked.

Zeb waved the comment away. No point in dwelling over should haves. 'How many of you are carrying?'

All of them were except Broker. 'I don't need guns. My brains are scary enough,' he said loftily.

Bwana and Roger collected the women's' handguns and their magazines under the cover of the table and distributed them.

'You got your earpieces?'

All of them had them. Gone were the days of speaking into a collar mic or a wrist mic.

These earpieces doubled as mic as well as speaker and were

near invisible. They weren't available commercially.

'Bear, Rog, Bwana, the four of us will conceal ourselves till these guys show our hand. We'll then play it by ear. Broker and the twins will be our eyes, at least in the restaurant.'

'Those two might have noticed the nine of us,' Beth objected.

'Which is where Yuri comes in. The moment we disappear, Yuri should show our SUV exiting the parking lot. That's their proof that we have left.'

'Broker, Yuri should loop the camera feed the moment these guys reveal themselves. That will lull them, will give us cover to move.'

'Where will you hide?' Meghan's voice was even, but the concern in her eyes was apparent.

Roger grinned, a smile that had captured many hearts from coast to coast and in many countries. 'It'll be hard for me since I stand out, naturally. These guys, they look like furniture. They'll be okay.'

'Ignore him,' Bear rumbled. 'We'll be fine. Chances are these guys will leave and we'll return, feeling foolish.'

None of them believed his last line. They all had finely-tuned inner senses. Each one's was pinging.

There was an immediate threat nearby.

Zeb went to the men's restroom.

Six stalls. Sink counter. No place to hide.

He turned to leave when his eyes drifted to the roof.

Suspended ceiling tiles.

He checked the stalls. They were empty. He locked the restroom from the inside, climbed on top of stall, drew out a dining knife and poked at one of the boards. It resisted, but gave way when he applied pressure.

He moved it cautiously and peered in the dark space.

It had pipes and tubing and AC ducts.

There was ample space for a body to lie.

He dropped down, unlocked the restroom, and took a swift look outside. No one was approaching it.

He climbed up the stall and squeezed through the small opening, drew in his legs and placed the tile back in place.

He inserted his knife in a crack between two tiles and widened it. Now he had eyes to the restroom.

Hopefully small enough to escape detection.

He waited. That was the easy part. He could wait for hours, days, weeks. Lie motionless for hours at end, just his eyes moving.

Waiting came naturally to him, to his men.

'I'm in,' he spoke softly. 'In the men's restroom.'

'So am I, in the laundry room.' Bear.

Bwana checked in. He was in a janitor's cupboard.

They waited a while for Roger to come in and when he did, they heard female voices in the background. 'Don't ask where, but my handsome self is hidden to the world.'

They waited. Zeb hoped the wait would be in vain and they could resume their celebrations.

Clare didn't do birthdays. The Agency was her life. It was precisely for that reason that the twins had planned the surprise get together.

Minutes merged. Men entered and exited the restroom. Toilets flushed.

Ninety minutes later, just when Zeb was thinking of overreaction, an assault rifle went off.

More firing followed, in different parts of the hotel. A stunned silence and then the screaming began.

'You were right. The same two guys in the dining room. No one killed. Not here, anyway.' Broker's voice was soft. Grim.

The beast in Zeb came to life. It filled him. It prepared him.

Unknown number of hostiles. More than a hundred hostages. Just four men to counter attack.

It was zero time.

Check out the rest of the Warriors Series

'Surely one of the best action writers of the day' Amazon review

On Amazon   On Amazon UK   On Nook   On Kobo   iTunes   On Ty's website

The Warrior

You are Zeb Carter, an agent with a deep black U.S. agency. You are a master of the killing game. In your business, the mission's rules are the only ones that matter. You break a cardinal one; and the game changes.

The Reluctant Warrior

Broker, the ace intelligence analyst in the Warriors crew, is good at finding things. Like finding people who don't want to be found. When an investigation goes wrong, he soon finds that hiding is far more difficult when he's the one who doesn't want to be found. Dying is increasingly certain when he's the one on the run.

The Warrior Code

All that Zeb Carter wants is to be left alone. The only thing Beth and Meghan Petersen want is an opportunity to rebuild their lives. All that a ruthless gang wants is to kill them all.

The Warrior's Debt

New York. Two killers. Both hunters. Neither of them is used to being prey.

Warriors Series Boxset, Books 1-4

Ex-Special Forces operative Zeb Carter works for a U.S. government agency that doesn't exist. You wouldn't remember him if you saw him. Those who are dying to meet him - get there.

These four thrillers are his stories. Over 900 pages of high-octane action and edge-of-your-seat mayhem that's perfect for today's thriller fans!

Flay

Zeb Carter has battled terrorists, mobsters, and despots in the most violent hotspots of the world. Nothing has prepared him for the Flayer, a serial killer in New York. The Flayer plans to break the internet. But that's only one part of his plan. The second part will break the city.

Behind You

They warned Elena Petrova to drop her story. She didn't. They raped her. She didn't give up. They killed her and buried her body where no man could find it. Unfortunately for them, one man did.

Zeb Carter is back. This time it's personal.

Author's Message

Thank you for taking time to read Hunting You. If you enjoyed it, please consider telling your friends and posting a short review.

Sign up to Ty Patterson's mailing list, and get The Warrior, free. Be the first to know about new releases and deals.

Ty's Amazon author page is here

The Warrior, Warriors series, Book 1

The Reluctant Warrior, Warriors series, Book 2

The Warrior Code, Warriors series, Book 3

The Warrior's Debt, Warriors series, Book 4

Warriors series Boxset, Books 1-4

Flay, Warriors series, Book 5

Behind You, Warriors series, Book 6

Hunting You, Warriors series, Book 7

About the Author

Ty has lived on a couple of continents and has been a trench digger, loose tea vendor, leather goods salesman, marine lubricants salesman, diesel engine mechanic, and is now an action thriller author.

Ty is privileged that readers of crime suspense and action thrillers have loved his books. 'Intense,' 'Riveting,' and 'Gripping' have been commonly used in reviews.

Ty lives with his wife and son, who humor his ridiculous belief that he's in charge.

Connect with Ty:

On Twitter
On Facebook
Website
Mailing list

CPSIA information can be obtained
at www.ICGtesting.com
Printed in the USA
LVOW12s1537030317

526084LV00002B/361/P

9 781523 211753